Monkey See, Monkey Zoo

Catch all the

ANIMAL TALES

Monkey See, Monkey Zoo

Erin Soderberg

illustrations by Guy Francis

BLOOMSBURY

NEW YORK BERLIN LONDON

For my silly little monkeys,
Milla, Henry, and Ruby

First published in the United States of America in September 2010
by Bloomsbury Books for Young Readers
www.bloomsburykids.com

For information about permission to reproduce selections from this book, write to
Permissions, Bloomsbury BFYR, 175 Fifth Avenue, New York, New York 10010

Library of Congress Cataloging-in-Publication Data
Soderberg, Erin.
Monkey see, monkey zoo / text by Erin Soderberg ; illustrations by Guy Francis. — 1st U.S. ed.
p.   cm.
Summary: After listening to a young boy describe his life, Willa the monkey escapes
from her zoo home and, together with some friendly chipmunks, goes in search of him
in the human city.
ISBN 978-1-59990-557-0 (hardcover) • ISBN 978-1-59990-558-7 (paperback)
[1. Monkeys—Fiction. 2. Zoos—Fiction. 3. City and town life—Fiction.]
I. Francis, Guy, ill. II. Title.
PZ7.S685257Mo 2010   [Fic]—dc22   2010008233

Book design by Danielle Delaney
Typeset by Westchester Book Composition
Printed in the U.S.A. by Worldcolor Fairfield, Pennsylvania
2 4 6 8 10 9 7 5 3 1 (hardcover)
2 4 6 8 10 9 7 5 3 1 (paperback)

All papers used by Bloomsbury Publishing, Inc., are natural, recyclable products
made from wood grown in well-managed forests. The manufacturing processes
conform to the environmental regulations of the country of origin.

Contents

The Treasure Collector

"Throwing grapes is not cool!" I screech this at the top of my lungs while readjusting my tiara. Then I shimmy across the branch and plop lightly onto the grass.

My brother, Timothy, is so immature.

I steal a peek back up in the tree; Timothy is still sitting there on our family branch, cackling and pointing at me. "Run, Willa, run!" he says and giggles, hopping and bouncing. He didn't actually hit me with one of his smushy little purple weapons—his aim is *very* bad—so I don't know what he thinks is so funny. It's as if the idea of grape bombs is hilarious or something. Grapes are a special treat, and Timothy is *wasting* them.

My mom says you should treasure your food, not waste it, since you never know where your next meal is coming from. Our Monkey Elders always say this—something about "the hunt" and scrounging for food in the wild. But I don't think we've ever *actually* had to worry about food in the Monkey Pit. Our human, Emily, comes three times every day, and it seems like she always *knows* the exact moment my tummy starts to grumble—so I think our Elders are just worry-warts.

I shake my head at Timothy again. He is now zinging his missiles at the rock below him to try to get them to explode, so I scoot over to my best friend ZuZu's rock. ZuZu hops a little bit to make room for me beside him, and I wrap my tail around him in greeting. "Are you watching that?" I ask, nodding toward Timothy. "Thank bananas he's starting school this year. Maybe he'll finally grow up and stop acting like such a baby."

ZuZu grins. He has the kind of face that's always grinning, just a little bit. That's why I like him so much. Also, he is always willing to trade

2

his apple for my banana at lunch. (I don't like the way banana smushes in with our monkey chow—when the dry brown pellets mix with banana, they make my fingers all goobery.) And once, ZuZu gave me half a cupcake that a human dropped over the fence into our Monkey Pit. *Ohhh . . . that was a tasty day.*

"Timothy is just doing Basic Skills this year, right?" ZuZu asks, and sticks his tongue out at my brother to blow a raspberry. Little pieces of banana shoot out of his mouth.

"Yep, Basic Skills. A beginner. He hasn't even been approved for rock hopping yet, so he definitely shouldn't be throwing things." I pick absent-mindedly at a patch of rough fur under my arm while carefully watching Timothy. His aim is actually getting better, and I don't want to be cleaning my fur all afternoon if he lands one of his missiles on me. Grapes are sticky little buggers.

When I hear laughter above me, I look up to see a group of three human girls staring down at us from the other side of the fence. I switch from picking to scratching under my arm and the girls laugh harder. I keep it up while I carry on the conversation with ZuZu—humans are easy. "Did you hear that Madame Rose Marie Osmond is teaching our class this year? I don't think I've ever even seen her do air acrobatics, so how is she going to *teach* it?" Madame Rose Marie Osmond is one of the Monkey Elders that spends a lot of time watching us and *tsk-tsk*ing, but I've never actually seen her land a backflip.

ZuZu doesn't say anything because he isn't listening to me. He's hopping and shouting silly things at the human girls, who are now howling with laughter. I can't help myself—it's too tempting to join in his fun. "Bug in a tutu! Chipmunks stink!"

Two cranky-looking women join the girls. They roll their eyes when they see what ZuZu and I are doing—Human Elders are always so prim and boring. I guess Monkey Elders are too. I think about Madame Rose Marie Osmond and my mom, two of our most serious Monkey Elders.

Come to think of it, none of Mom's friends ever do anything except chatter about what to have for lunch. I don't know why they bother worrying about it, since there's never really any choice. We take what Emily brings us, and that's the end of it. My mom always acts like it's this big sacrifice

to gather lunch for the family. But come on, it arrives at the Monkey Pit on a tray, cut up and everything!

ZuZu and I spend a few more minutes shouting things at the human girls, until each of their Elders takes them by the arm and leads them into a part of the human cage that I can't see.

"ZuZu, have you ever wondered how big the human cage is?" I ask my best friend. "If you think about it, every single day, hundreds of humans wander past the Monkey Pit, right? Big ones, little ones, mean ones, silly ones . . . there are, like, a *million* people."

He nods, but I can tell he's distracted, watching a kid who can't figure out how to get the straw from his juice box into his mouth. ZuZu's lips pucker, as if to show the little human how it's done. I keep talking anyway. "Even if the human cage is ten times bigger than our cage, I *still* don't know how they all fit in there!"

"Maybe they just smush together and cuddle a lot?" ZuZu suggests. He's busy peeling another banana. ZuZu is a really sneaky guy, and somehow he always gets away with an extra banana or two at mealtime. He doesn't take them just because he's extra hungry—even though he always *is* extra hungry. He saves them for later because he likes to do tricks with 'nanas when humans are watching.

Sometimes ZuZu will put the whole fruit of the banana in his mouth, then slap his hands against his cheeks so the banana bits all come flying out. Another trick he loves is squeezing an unopened banana with his hand until the pressure forces the fruit part inside to come shooting out of its skin like a mushy worm. That's the trick he's working on now, but the 'nana skin is extra tough today, so he's not having a lot of luck. He asks, "Do you think in the human cage, they all have their own covered dens, like we do? Or do you think they sleep outside?"

I shake my head. It's a good question. I've never been outside the Monkey Pit fence, but I've always wondered how big the neighboring zoo cage is—the one that holds the humans. People are a lot bigger than monkeys, but it doesn't seem fair that their cage is obviously so large. I wish I knew what they do in there all day—they seem to have a lot of time to stand and stare at us, that's for sure.

The Monkey Pit is pretty nice, I guess. I don't have anything to compare it to, but they give us lots of toys and we're hardly ever hungry. We have a stream and a little pond surrounded by big stones that we can sit on to relax and dry off in the sun. There are a bunch of trees, and each tree is assigned to a few monkey families. My family's branch is right next to ZuZu's family's, and another girl from our class—Delilah Delilah the Third—hangs with her family on one of the branches farther up in the tree. We also have a Basic Skills area with balls and ropes, and the agility course where my Air Acrobatics class will be held.

The cushiest parts of our Monkey Pit are the underground tunnels with each family's sleeping den. When it rains, my mom usually makes me stay inside our den so I don't stink of wet fur. She's really picky that way. Also, it hurts when she has to pluck the tangles out of my fluffy hair, and rain is the *worst* for stirring up tangles.

"Princess Willoughby Wallaby Fluff!" At the sound of my full name, I jump up and scamper across the rocks that line the perimeter of the Pit, heading toward my family den. My mom is the only monkey who ever uses my full name. Everyone else just calls me Willa. "Miss Fluff, can you please explain this?" My mom is holding one hand toward me and something sparkles in her palm.

It's my new treasure.

It's shiny and magical and I thought I'd hid it well enough that she wouldn't find it. "It's an earring," I explain. "A dangly earring." *Purple and wonderful and* mine*! How did she find it?*

"Yes," Mom says, and nods. "I see that it's an earring. Where, precisely, did you get it?"

"From the ledge." The earring that I snatched from the ledge yesterday is just one of the millions of treasures the humans are hiding over in their cage. I love human treasures. . . . There are hats and balloons and piles of treats that fall from the human cage into ours. As I think about treats my tummy rumbles, and I wonder when Emily will be here with lunch.

Mom snorts angrily. *Uh-oh.* "Willa, I thought we'd discussed this. You are not to climb up to the ledge of the Monkey Pit. Didn't we come to an understanding about this last week? The ledge is very dangerous, and you could fall. We belong *in* the Monkey Pit—if the zookeepers wanted us to jump around up on the ledge, they would have built a staircase. But they didn't, so you need to keep your tail out of the humans' business. Do you understand?"

I blink slowly, putting one hand squarely atop my tiara—my most prized possession. I don't want to risk it being taken from me as punishment. Because, in fact, my mom *had* mentioned that she didn't want me to climb up to the ledge of the Monkey Pit again. But I hadn't exactly *agreed* to her terms.

The ledge runs along the uppermost edge of the Pit, just below the fence. At least once a week, one of the humans drops a treasure of some kind over the fence between their cage and ours, and it lands on the ledge. *Someone* has to gather up those treasures. It is my *duty*. I consider myself the official treasure collector.

"Willa?" Mom licks her finger and reaches out to smooth the fur above my ear.

"I'm sorry, Mom." My mom nods, soothed, and I can't believe I am actually going to get away with a simple apology. She's usually much sterner than this—maybe she thinks the earring is as beautiful as I do, and that it was worth a trip to the ledge. I really ought to keep an eye out for a special treasure for my mom. . . . She would probably like something soft, like a sock. "Does that mean I get to keep the earring?"

"Are you going to climb up to the ledge again?" She's still holding the earring and doesn't look enthusiastic about the idea of giving it back to me. She leans toward me to catch a little fly that just landed on my arm, and pops it into her mouth.

"I will try very hard not to." I push my lips out and try to look trustworthy. But I'm crossing my arms behind my back, because there's no way I'm not going up to the ledge again—I already know that. I'm always very careful. Really.

Mom is still staring at me with the earring draped across her palm when Timothy comes scampering into our den. I decide to turn Mom on Timothy to take some of the heat off me. Maybe she'll forget she's mad at me and drop the earring. "Mom, can you tell Timothy he's not supposed to throw his food?"

My mom wraps her fingers around my treasure and turns to Timothy—*backfire! She still has the earring in her hand!* "What am I going to do with the two of you? Thank bananas school is starting tomorrow. A little structure and time apart will do you both a lot of good." Then, still holding my earring, she shuffles off to gather lunch.

"Mom, where are you going with my purple dangly earring?" I call desperately. She ignores me. I realize it will take a lot of creativity for me to convince Mom to return the earring to my treasure box. More than likely, it will take a plan.

I set off in search of ZuZu, my partner in plan-plotting action. Oh, sparkly treasure, you will be mine again!

The Human Zoo

I find ZuZu dangling way up at the tippy-top of the tickling tree. We call it the tickling tree because it has all these scraggly branches that reach out and grab you when you're climbing up to the best perch. The branches are like funny little fingers that get twisted up in my fur and poke at all the squishy spots. I'm super ticklish. Usually, if anyone even looks under my arms, I start laughing because I can't help but think about being tickled under there.

As I climb up to meet ZuZu, the branches scratch at my face and arms and toes, and I laugh and hoot and holler. Of course, this makes all of the humans in their cage crack up, which makes ZuZu giggle, and then we're all having a great time.

Summer is the best. All through the hot months, the zoo is filled with human kids and ZuZu and I get to hang around all day, listening to them talk about cool stuff. They also cheer when we do tricks, which is pretty sweet.

When I plunk down on the branch next to ZuZu, he's swinging his legs through the air, holding fast to the branch with only his hands. "You are getting really good at that," I say. "Try it one-handed!"

ZuZu drops one hand and swings slowly at first, then faster. "Madame Rose Marie Osmond won't even know what to do with me—I'm a talent. An Air Acrobatics superstar! I am the monkey star of the zoo. Watch me go! Swing, ZuZu, swing!"

Just as he announces this, looking boastfully at the humans, ZuZu's hand slips, and he falls from the branch. He lands squarely on his feet on the next perch down. I squeeze my lips together to keep from laughing. "That was great," I tease.

ZuZu is always showing off.
He got hurt a lot when we
were in Basic Skills,
and I'm nervous for
class to start this
year. ZuZu can be
a little careless, and
Air Acrobatics is
too dangerous to be
showing off all the
time. "I really liked
the end of that trick,
the part where you
flew off the branch. Did
you plan that?"

"Absolutely!" ZuZu lies. Then he hops up and
down on the branch below me, shaking the whole
tree in an effort to make me lose my balance too.
I curl my toes and hands around the branch and
hold tight. When he sees that I'm not going to fall,
he scrambles up past the tickly branches and sits
next to me. "You missed a good conversation a
few minutes ago," he says, breathless.

I cluck my tongue. "Really? About what?" Our
favorite thing about this branch is that it is way up

in the sky, close to the top of the Monkey Pit, so we can hear a lot of what the humans talk about. It gets boring listening to monkey chatter all day, and humans say funny things sometimes. We learn a lot about the zoo on the other side of our fence this way too.

"A girl sitting in one of those rolling carts was talking about something called a 'dog.' It sounded furry, and the girl said it licks stuff with its tongue. Maybe it's some sort of cleaning product?"

"Like a cleaning animal? I need a cleaning animal for my fur—my mom tugs too hard when she cleans me." I prefer baths in the pond, but sometimes stuff gets too stuck in my fluffy hair for me to get it out myself.

"Yeah, I'll bet that's what it is. A cleaning animal." ZuZu reaches over to grab a gnat that is crawling across my shoulders. He sucks it into his mouth with a giant slurp. "Anyway, it sounded like this 'dog' thing lives in the human's house. I wonder why we've never seen one come past the fence."

I shrug. "The humans hide a lot from us." It's true. They are always talking about the food they get to eat and their freedom to see all the other animals at the zoo. I think they're worse than birds, sometimes, with all their bragging. But unlike birds, who fly off and then report back on the adventures they've had, all we ever see humans do is stand at the fence and look at us. Monkeys are really interesting, so the humans are lucky.

Honestly, I sometimes get bored of sharing a fence with the humans. They don't do many tricks that are fun to watch—they just sort of talk and stand there. I wish we shared a fence with the seals. From what the humans say about the seals at the zoo, I get the impression they're pretty neat (I heard a human say seals can balance balls on their noses, so I've been working on that trick too).

"Oh, get this," I say, remembering the reason I set out to find ZuZu in the first place. "My mom busted me for going up to the ledge again, and she says I definitely can't go up there anymore. She found the earring."

"The purple dangly one?" ZuZu asks, curling and uncurling his toes around the tree's branch.

"Yes!" I cry. "We need a plan—a plan to get it back from her."

"*Ooh! Ooh!* I love plans." ZuZu is hopping and shimmying on the branch. He's famous for his plans. Of course, I already know this, which is why I came to him for help. ZuZu is the one who came up with the idea of hiding all our balls inside the sleeping dens so the zookeepers would have to bring us *more* to play with—now we have enough balls for everyone! Another time, he figured out how to connect two branches together on one of our trees to create a little swing. And even though he'd never admit it now, he came up with the original plan that got me up to the ledge the first time . . . the day I collected my shiny tiara!

I shimmy with him, curling my tail around his. "Here's what I was thinking—I bet if I got my mom a special present, she would forget all about the dangly earring and I could get it back. Also, I just know my mom would love something special from the human cage; something just for her. She'd look really pretty with a soft sock on her arm or with a shiny headband in her hair. Mom loves pink."

"How are you going to get your mom a present if you can't go to the ledge anymore?" ZuZu asks, squinting his eyes and bunching up his face at me. "You're not really going to disobey your mom, are you?"

I guess that's a good question. "I don't think it

counts if I go to the ledge to get something special for Mom. She wouldn't mind one more little treasure-collecting trip, as long as I bring her a special something, right?"

"Good point." ZuZu agrees. "I think your mom would be happy to have a present. I'm sure she would understand, just this time." He squeezes his face into a pucker, and I can tell he's thinking through plans in his head. He really loves to plot. "*Ooh, ooh!* I know! Maybe you can make a human laugh so hard that they'll stop paying attention and drop something *really* good."

That's a good idea, I think, nodding. When human kids get distracted, they sometimes drop their stuff. That's always how we get special human-food treats, like cookies and hot dog buns. "Maybe if we're extra funny, they'll drop a few things, so I can get a new treasure too. Maybe a spoon or something fun like that! And maybe we'll get lucky and they'll drop a snack for you."

"I would like a special human snack." ZuZu grins, then he pinches his lips together again. "But, Willa, you have so many human treasures now that there's hardly anywhere left for you to hide them. Do you really need more stuff for you?"

"You don't understand," I say, pouting. "Collecting treasures is the way I learn about things."

"You learn about things by disobeying all of our Elders and going up to the ledge?" ZuZu is grinning, teasing me. "You'd better be careful, or you're going to get caught in the act! You'd probably be better off just going out into the human part of the zoo to explore. We can't fit any more of your treasures in the Monkey Pit!"

I blow a raspberry at him and hop on the branch to show that I'm not afraid to bounce him right off if he keeps teasing me. I don't know why I get into so much trouble for going to the ledge— other monkeys are much naughtier than I am.

Take ZuZu, for instance: he's always doing tricks that we haven't been certified to do yet. As young monkeys, we have to get approved to do things like hang from our tails and even swing upside down. Most of the adult monkeys are allowed to do whatever tricks they want, but kids get in trouble if we're caught testing out the coolest moves before we pass our classes with a "Good" or "Excellent" grade.

"What am I supposed to do? Just leave everything up on the ledge, lost and forgotten?"

ZuZu blows a raspberry. "Your tiara is cool, but

you don't even play with any of your other trea-sures because you're afraid someone's going to find them and take them from you."

"That's not true!" Sometimes I pretend to be asleep at night, and when the rest of my family is snoring, I get up and pull all my treasures out of their hiding places. Then I line everything up and look at it, counting and organizing and imagining what I would do with each prize if I didn't have to hide everything from the zookeepers and my mom.

I like to imagine what the humans do with all that stuff over in their cage. Do they actually *use* all of the wonderful treasures that they have in their cage? Is it possible that they love them as much as I do?

I like to think that maybe, someday, I'll find out.

Carter and His Treasure Pack

ZuZu and I are still bouncing and poking at each other on our branch, talking about our plan to get my mom a present, when a quiet boy wearing a colorful backpack comes right up to the fence and stares at us. His big eyes peer through the branches at the edge of the Monkey Pit. He stands there staring, just watching us watching him. ZuZu and I stop talking about my treasures and exchange a look, wondering when he'll get bored and move on to watch someone else. Neither of us is doing anything very interesting at the moment.

Suddenly, the little boy grins and says, "Hi, monkeys."

"Hi. I'm Willa," I answer, touching my tiara proudly. "Actually, it's Princess Willoughby Wallaby Fluff, but most people just call me Willa. This is my best friend, ZuZu."

The boy takes off his backpack and sets it against the fence in front of him. I notice that one of the straps is poking through the bottom of the fence, so close to where I could reach it if I jumped over to the ledge. It's tempting to do that; just snatch the backpack from him. It would look really good on my back. The boy speaks again. "I'm Carter."

"I like that name!" I say happily. "And I love your backpack. Do you have anything good in there?"

"I've always wanted to ask one of you monkeys something," Carter says, ignoring me. It's as if he couldn't even understand my question. "Do you go to school too?"

I clap and nod. "Tomorrow ZuZu and I are going to be starting Air Acrobatics. My brother, Timothy, will be in Basic Skills. That's just the beginner class."

Carter grins. "You sure screech a lot. You're a funny monkey," he says, but I don't really know what's so funny about Air Acrobatics *or* Basic Skills. And I'm not *screeching*, I'm *talking*. Is he even listening to what I'm saying? "I bet you must go to school. Everyone goes to school, right?"

ZuZu and I both jump up and down and shimmy on the branch to show Carter some of the things we learned last year in Basic Skills.

Carter's toe kicks his backpack and it slides even farther under the fence. I eye it up and down. I want it *so* badly. This would be the treasure to beat all other treasures, a treasure pack that could hold all of my other prized finds and keep them safe. Of course, this isn't the right thing to give my mom, but I'll definitely keep an eye out for something good for her too.

If I had Carter's backpack, I would wear it on my back every day, keeping my treasures close. Carter speaks again, distracting me from my backpack dreams. "I'm starting third grade tomorrow. At Lakeside Elementary School. It's not actually on a lake, so I don't know why they call it that."

I laugh. Carter is funny. I like that he's talking *to* us, instead of just talking *about* us to one of his friends or his dad. Carter seems to be alone, and I wonder where his Elders are. Usually, the young humans bring an Elder with them to the fence.

"We do really cool stuff, like reading and math, and this year we're going to do a project with clay—I think I might make a clay monkey. Or maybe an elephant." My eyes widen, wondering what an elephant is. It sounds scary.

Carter is chatting happily and quickly, telling ZuZu and me all about his school. "I even heard we might get to make an exploding volcano that erupts and sprays stuff all over the classroom." Carter is talking louder now, getting even more excited about Lakeside Elementary and this volcano thing.

"We also have show-and-tell once a week, where everyone brings something that's special to them and shares it with the class." Carter looks a little like Timothy when he gets excited—both of their arms wiggle wildly in the air, as if they're blowing around in the wind. "Nakita Jackson brought in her pet ferret last year when we were in second grade—it was so cool."

I turn to look at ZuZu, who is wearing the same wide-eyed expression I am. I mutter under my breath, "This place sounds perfect. Show-and-tell? Exploding volcanoes? I don't know what volcanoes are, but they sound so exciting! Maybe it's food?"

"Yeah," ZuZu murmurs back. "Carter's school sounds way cooler than Air Acrobatics with Madame Rose Marie Osmond."

Carter is still talking, listing off all kinds of things they do in third grade. "Oh, and I just got this backpack from my grandpa," he says, pointing at the backpack on the ground. "It's my special school backpack. My house is only a couple blocks away from school, so Grandma usually walks me there, and I put all my school stuff in my pack. Check this out—I also have my first show-and-tell in here already! It's a rock with crystals inside that I got from my uncle this summer. I'm going to bring it to school tomorrow to show everyone."

Carter unzips the backpack to show us a little gray rock with sparkling white crystals nestled inside. It looks magical, and it is beyond a doubt the most beautiful thing I've ever seen—even more beautiful than my tiara or the purple earring. He holds the rock in his hand for a few seconds, then plops it back in his backpack and zips up the pouch. "Do you take backpacks to your school?"

I blow air out from between my lips. *I wish.*

"Lakeside Elementary is great. When I get to sixth grade, I have to go to Barton Middle School. It's farther away from my house, so I'll take the school bus."

Carter keeps talking, but I lean over toward ZuZu and ask, "What's a school bus?"

"Beats me," he whispers back.

"Lakeside School is really close to the library, so sometimes my grandma takes me there after school so I can pick out a book. She even some-times stops to get me ice cream at Frank's. I like chocolate-banana ice cream. Hey! I bet you'd like chocolate-banana ice cream. Frank makes the best ice cream in the world."

"*Ooh! Ooh!*" I shout. "That sounds great." I have no idea what ice cream is, but I like ice and I like cream—and anything with bananas is deli-cious!

Carter laughs. "Maybe sometime I'll try to sneak some into the zoo for you. But don't tell any-one."

Just as I'm about to answer, someone yells, "Carter! We need to get a move on!" Our human buddy smiles at us again, then dashes off into the part of the human cage we can't see, even from the top branches.

"Good luck in third grade!" I call after him, then turn to my best friend. "ZuZu, this Lakeside Elementary place sounds incredible. I want to go to human school. I bet I could get a great present for my mom there and everything."

"I need to get some of that chocolate-banana ice-cream stuff Carter was talking about." ZuZu rubs his stomach, and it growls in response. "Frank must be the human's zookeeper. I can't believe the humans get this thing called ice cream, and they give us fruit and monkey chow every day? We should tell Emily that *we* want banana ice cream in our meal delivery! I'm sure I would love it."

I turn back to the fence and notice something. "ZuZu, look!"

ZuZu screeches. "Oh no! Carter's backpack!"

I feel this sudden excitement deep in the pit of my belly. "Carter forgot his school backpack. He *needs* his backpack for school. He needs his treasure for show-and-tell!" I know just how Carter will feel when he realizes he's lost his special treasure—just the same way I felt when my mom took my purple earring.

ZuZu's stomach growls again. "What are we going to do?" he asks nervously, already knowing what I have in mind.

"I'm going up to the ledge," I say, without even thinking about it for a second. "I need to rescue Carter's backpack."

Escape!

The climb up to the ledge is steep and dangerous. I guess that's why it's off-limits. But I got an
"Excellent" during the climbing unit in Basic
Skills last year. My teacher, Fred Astaire, said I
am a natural climber. And I am always super
careful.

I look up at the top of the tree and measure the
distance from the edge of the jumping branch to
the ledge. It always looks like such a wide expanse,
but when I get there and take the plunge, the
jump is a cinch. As I size it up today, ZuZu follows
my gaze. "Don't do it, Willa. You're going to get

into so much trouble. Your mom is already way too mad at you today."

"No one will know," I say, but I don't necessarily believe that. "Carter needs his backpack."

ZuZu stares at me. "But wouldn't it be better if you just left it there for Carter to come back and get it?"

I can't believe I'm actually saying this, but I hear it come out of my mouth. "I'm going to go over the fence. I'm going to bring Carter's backpack to him!"

"You're going *in* the human cage?" ZuZu starts shouting, and some of the monkeys sitting below us are suddenly looking up, curious. "I was kidding when I told you to do that before. Willa, that's against all the rules."

I set my lips in a solid line and wrap my tail around ZuZu's back fondly. "It will be easy," I say confidently. "I'll find Carter, give him his backpack, pick up a great present for my mom, and maybe take a quick peek at Lakeside Elementary. A tiny little glimpse, just to see what human school is like."

"But monkeys don't go into the human cage. We don't cross the fence."

"Not usually," I agree. "But this is not a usual

situation. Carter is our friend. We have to help him. He *needs* his backpack for school." Okay, I'll admit it . . . I'm also very, very interested in seeing what the human cage is like. I've never been anywhere except the Monkey Pit my whole life, and I know there's a whole zoo out there, waiting to be explored. Think of all the treasures! Think of the cool stuff I could bring to show-and-tell! Think of the presents I could choose from to bring back to my mom! "ZuZu, if I lost one of my treasures, I know you'd help me make a plan to get it back. We have to do the same for Carter. It's what friends do."

"You're going to do this whether or not I think it's a good idea, aren't you?" ZuZu still looks worried, but I see that familiar grin widening on his face and there is a glint of mischief in his eyes.

"Yep."

"I'll help you," he promises. "I'll distract the Elders."

"But then you might get in trouble too. You'd do that for me?" I ask.

"Of course. You're my best friend. But, um, Willa?" He looks sheepish. "Can you try to get me some of that ice cream while you're in the human cage?"

I hug my tail tighter around ZuZu's back and laugh. "Sure."

"Banana?"

"Definitely."

"Do you want to go now, or wait until after lunch?" ZuZu asks.

I know ZuZu expects me to eat first, so I think I surprise him when I say, "I need to get going now. There's still a chance for me to catch Carter. He must still be close, right? Then maybe he can show me the way to Lakeside Elementary and I'll be back in time for dinner. Save me an apple from lunch?"

ZuZu nods, then points up to the top of the tree and whispers, "Go for it. Good luck, Willa!"

And with that little burst of confidence from my best friend, I reach my hands up the trunk of the tree, pull myself upward, and swing out onto the spindly jumping branch. I creep a toe forward, then my whole foot.

What am I doing? I wonder briefly as the branch bends under my weight. Then I remember Carter, and everything he told us about school and his backpack, and I pull my other leg forward. *I need to bring his backpack to him. Even Mom would understand this time.* I feel the branch drop as I bring more of my weight forward, toward the edge.

I risk a quick glance down, and I see that ZuZu is dangling from the lower arm of the tickling tree, preparing to swing across branches all the way to his family branch. He's shouting and cackling, attracting stares and *tsk-tsk*ing from the Elders. Everyone who is sitting around outside waiting for lunch is busy watching ZuZu, and no one is paying attention to me up at the top of the tree.

My foot slips, and I'm forced to grab the branch with my hands to steady myself. I get a rush of fear and excitement, then creep forward one more step. My plan is to take the first jump to the ledge, then shimmy along the edge a few feet, where I can climb up and over the fence.

I think the zookeepers believe we can't jump out of the Monkey Pit, but the reality is that no monkey has ever wanted to before—at least, not that I know about. So no one has ever tried. I've never truly considered actually leaving my world before—even just for a quick visit to the other side—but that's because no one has ever told me the human cage has clay and show-and-tell and ice cream.

I suddenly want, more than anything, to know what's on the other side. I want to know what's happening in the rest of the zoo. I *need* to know, and I need to find Carter.

Just as my foot scoots the last few inches to the very edge of the branch, I hear Timothy's little voice shout up at me from the lower branches of the tickling tree. He must have hopped off our family branch and run along the edge of the Monkey Pit to find me. He screeches, "Willa, your lunch is ready."

But it's too late to pause, so my body tenses and I make the leap, flying through the air to the ledge. I land soundly on the solid surface, my foot touching Carter's backpack strap. I pull the pack through the space under the fence and loop the shoulder strap across my arm. "Willa, stop!" It's Timothy again, and I realize he sounds scared.

His fear creeps under my fur, and I wonder if I should listen to my little brother. *I can't do this*, I think. As I let my nerves take hold, I feel my foot slip, and I grab the fence with my free hand.

It's now or never, I tell myself, knowing that I need to make a move or I'm going to fall. I take a deep breath, and my foot stretches sideways on the ledge, toward the section of the fence I can shimmy over.

"Willa, what are you doing?" Timothy cries this with his loudest voice, and I hear the gasps from other monkeys as my foot and hand reach together over the top of the fence, and my body slides easily up and onto the other side.

I peek down into the Monkey Pit from outside the fence and grin like crazy.

Then I take a deep breath and strap Carter's pack on my shoulders. I shout, "Hello, down there!" and wave at my brother before turning away from the Monkey Pit for my first look inside the human cage.

Carter, I'm on my way!

Zoo Skidoo

"Whoa," I mutter, taking it all in. The human cage is crazy-big. A million times bigger than the Monkey Pit. I can't even see the other side of the humans' fence from where I'm crouching, low and out of sight. All I can see is people everywhere, holding cups and pushing those rolling carts that Human Elders push around with smaller humans in them. There is some sort of agility station where kids are climbing and swinging and riding down shiny platforms.

Watching the kids play and leap and swing in the agility station makes me think of ZuZu's tree-branch swing. I bet there's a human kid who likes to come up with fun plans just as much as ZuZu does. I love watching the kids swing and slide, and I really wish we had a view of this agility station from inside the Monkey Pit—it's the first time I've ever seen humans actually doing cool tricks, not just standing there, staring at me and my monkey friends.

I creep a foot forward and get a good view of some humans sitting on funny seats, eating lunch. One little human—it's one of the extra-small baby humans without much hair—is throwing its food on the ground. I giggle when his Elder tells him to stop. Just like my mom and Timothy!

I stand there for a minute or so, hiding behind a large container, before I really, truly realize what I've just done. I have left the Monkey Pit.

I'm free—an escaped monkey, loose in the zoo!

"*Ooh! Ooh!*" I cry, excited and nervous and unable to stay quiet. Then I peek out from behind the container again and wonder, *What now?*

First things first, I know I probably need to be sneaky. No other animals have ever been in the Monkey Pit before (except birds, who have free run of the zoo, and sometimes those really annoying squirrels and chipmunks, who like to think they're monkeys). This makes me think I am not very welcome over here in the human cage. Otherwise, why would they have the fences around all of us?

In addition to stealth, I need to have speed. Carter walked away from the Monkey Pit at least ten minutes ago, so I need to hustle if I'm going to find him. I secure his pack on my back, check to make sure my tiara is in place, and move. I move faster than I've ever moved before.

My legs fly across a path, right in front of a bunch of kids. They point and shout, and I grin at them over my shoulder as I zip forward. By the time their Elders turn to look, I'm out of sight, a poof of fur that's practically invisible.

I scoot through grassy areas, squeezing between obstacles and benches in a flash. I pass a big fence that has two giant green monsters on the other side. "*Ayee!*" I screech, turning as fast as I can to get away from the creatures. I sneak a quick look back over my shoulder and see the monsters opening their giant mouths. I've never seen teeth like that! That *cannot* be real!

"Hey, monkey!" I hear a bird squawk from over

my shoulder. I stop for just a moment, long enough to hear the bird chirp, "Alligators love monkeys— *snip-snap!*" This makes me run even faster. Because those alligators . . . they're scary!

When I pass the next fence, I poke around a human's legs to see a swatch of soft white fur curled up at the back of this animal pit. I hear a Human Elder call the thing a polar bear. I peek for another quick minute and decide that bears look nice. Cuddly. I think I would like to be friends with a bear. And then I'm off again, out of sight and out of reach.

When I spot a giant pond up ahead, I'm so tempted to stop for a quick swim. All this running is making me hot and sticky in the late-summer sun. But as I get closer, I realize there are all these slippery-looking dark things inside the pond. They're like giant black worms with funny flat arms. They sound like sick monkeys. My eyes bulge, staring at these crazy floating beasts. No way am I going swimming in this pond. As I watch, one of the creatures pops out of the water and bounces a ball on its nose—seals! These are the funny seals the humans talk about!

I hear someone call out "Monkey!" and realize

I better scoot off on my way. In seconds, I'm up a tree, flying through the branches, looking down from the treetops as I zoom farther and farther through the human cage.

This place is unbelievable! Huge, and filled with trees and benches and little shelves stacked with food. I stop to rest at the top of a tree to survey my surroundings and search for Carter from up above. I can't see him anywhere, but I do smell something delicious just below me. I peek through the branches and see soft bread circles, stuffed inside small white paper bags. My stomach rumbles, and I know I *need* those bread circles.

I scuttle down the branches until I'm just above the bags filled with soft bread circles. They smell sweet and wonderful. "Why do the humans get so much variety in their meal delivery?" I wonder aloud. We get our monkey chow (Emily's special name for boring old brown pellets), fruit, and sometimes veggies. Once a week they give us raisins with honey. But bread circles? Nope, never.

The branch creaks under my weight as I wrap my legs around the lowest branch and snake myself down toward the little shelf, reaching out a

hand for one of the bags of dough circles. I stretch, my fingers just close enough to graze the tops of the bags, before finally finding one I can pinch between my fingers.

I settle into a comfy spot in the tree, scratching my back fur on the bark of the tree's trunk. Then I pluck the first bread circle—*hello, delicious!*—out of the bag. A gold and brown bird that has been sitting beside me in the tree flutters over and snaps off a piece of the dough circle with its beak.

I pull the bag away from the pest, then hold the sweet-smelling bread under my nose and sniff. "*Ohhhh,*" I sigh. It smells like honey. I poke my lips out to touch the soft dough circle. I can't control my mouth and it opens quickly, snatching up the treat. I barely chew the first one before the second, then third, fourth, and finally the whole bag are in my mouth.

"I wubb dough wircles!" I cry through a mouthful of sugar. Then I burp and my stomach growls. Not the comfortable growling sound of hunger slipping away, but a rumbling, icky feeling.

The bird sizes me up. "Those are called *dough-nuts.* Everyone knows it's not a good idea to eat a whole bag of doughnuts by yourself, monkey. You're supposed to peck delicately, just tasting them."

"My *name* is Willa, and I would have appreciated your advice *before* I ate the whole bag," I grumble, my stomach tossing and turning.

The bird chirps rudely, then flies off, leaving me alone again.

I'm still moaning about my poor tummy when I see him. *Carter!* He's walking toward a giant flat space, filled with colored metal creatures. Some of the creatures are moving, and people are sitting inside them. The bird is back, pecking at the crumbs inside my doughnut bag, so I ask, "What are those things?" I point to the creatures, which are all kinds of colors and sizes and shapes.

"Cars," the bird tweets, giggling. "The humans use them to drive home."

"Home?" I ask, ignoring the bird's laughter. Birds are so frustrating. They think they're so superior, with their wings and their endless freedom to go anywhere. But they can't dangle, and monkeys can. Thinking about this makes me feel better. "Isn't their home here?"

"The zoo?" the bird asks, distracted by my

doughnut crumbs. "No, only animals live at the zoo, silly. Humans live in the city."

"How do they get to the city?" I ask, suddenly panicked. *Humans don't live at the zoo?*

The bird looks at me the way I sometimes look at Timothy. It's not a very nice look. "They take a car or a bus. If you were a bird, you could fly there. But if you have to run like, say, a monkey, it would take you a whole day to get there."

I can still see Carter way off in the distance, walking through the mass of cars. I need to catch him before he gets in a car! I scramble quickly down the tree and run, run, run.

Monkey Bike

Get this: the zoo is bigger than huge. I realized I was somewhere much bigger than the Monkey Pit from the moment I squirmed over the edge of the fence. But now that I'm running past crowds of people and shops and agility stations and fountains and animals, I realize I *definitely* underestimated its size. I'm actually feeling exhausted as I leap and bound through the zoo. We don't have to climb or run this far to get to anything in our Pit, and it seems I may be a slower runner than I thought I was!

It doesn't help that I have to keep popping up

into trees to reset myself on the right track. And climbing is harder than it looks. From way up high in the treetops, it looks like the car things are *just* over there, but *aha!* The zoo people are tricky! There are fences and trees and buildings and garbage cans and hot dog carts standing in the way of the easiest path to the cars, so it takes a bit of planning to map my course. Good thing we learned *bounding* in Basic Skills.

As I run, I can hear people calling to me, yelling, "Monkey, monkey! Stop!" I have a feeling they're trying to steal my tiara as punishment for going up to the ledge, so I run faster every time someone comes toward me. I feel a hand clutch at my tail, but I shake it off, scampering up into a tree just in time. They're not going to get my tiara! And no way are they going to take Carter's backpack from me!

When I finally get to the place where the cars are kept, the big field is overwhelming. It's as if I'm swimming in a sea of colored car creatures. The hot ground burns my feet, and I long for the coolness of the monkey stream. I can no longer smell the fresh leaves and flowers that blow through the air inside the Monkey Pit—instead, it just smells sort of hot and it feels like cars are squeezing against me.

I realize I better scamper across the *tops* of the cars or I'm going to get lost in the maze. Also, there are people walking everywhere and the cars are moving! These car creatures are much bigger than monkeys or humans, so I'm really scared that one will chase me and bite my backside.

As I scramble up the front of a car—keeping a close eye out for teeth or claws—I realize the brown and gold bird has followed me, and now she won't stop chirping. It's as though the bird is trying to confuse me. *Ugh*, birds.

I skitter across a big brown car, then hop up on a tall blue one that is big enough for me to have a great view of everything. I begin to scan the field of cars, briefly distracted by a really soft-looking pretend bird that is hanging from a mirror inside the car I'm sitting on—I'd like to have it. It would look really flashy around my neck or tucked under my arm.

There!

I spot Carter, now just a speck off in the distance, farther away from me than the Monkey Pit is wide. He's with his Elder, and they're holding hands. I'm getting ready to let out a screech, loud and long, but I open my mouth and suck in a breath moments too late. Carter has just opened the door to a blue car and it closes behind him as my monkey howl fills the field of cars. "Carter! Stop! I have your backpack!"

Suddenly, there is noise everywhere. Humans are gawking at me, stopping in their cars to point and stare. Elders are shouting, kids are laughing, and people are running in circles—it's as though they've never seen a monkey before. I ignore all of them and fly over the tops of cars as fast as I can toward Carter, trying to catch the car creature he's riding in before it rolls away. The annoying bird flutters behind me, taunting. "They're going to get you," the bird cheeps. "These humans are going to catch you! You're not allowed to be out of the Monkey Pit."

I ignore her, my heart pounding as I tear through the maze of cars. The shouts of humans behind me fade as I reach the edge of the cars—I'm too fast for them to catch me, but not fast enough to catch Carter. When I get to the place where it had stood just moments before, Carter's blue car is gone, rolling away toward the edge of the human cage. As the car pulls up to the edge of the fence, a big gate opens and the blue car disappears behind the gates. I don't know what's behind that fence, but I am pretty sure that Carter has just left the zoo.

What am I going to do now? I worry. I can feel the weight of the backpack on my shoulders, and I think about Carter's rock, nestled inside the front pocket. Then I think about his books, and Carter's poor, tired arms carrying them all the way from his house to school tomorrow. He needs his backpack! But I know the bird was right—I'll never catch that car. Cars are way faster than any monkey, probably faster than birds, even.

The annoying bird lands on my tiara and I shake my head to try to get her to fly away. I don't need her here right now. I need to think, and the weight of her sticky brown and gold feathers is heavy on top of my head. As I hop, trying to force the doughnut-thieving annoyance off my tiara, I see my opportunity.

Just a few feet away, a small green car has just started to roll out of the spot it had been sleeping in. Right there, on the back of the car, a bike is hanging from a metal rack. Sometimes I see human kids riding bikes around the zoo.

I leap before I can consider the decision, squeezing my body onto one of the bike pedals, and wrap my arms and legs around the bike as the car rolls away from the zoo. I tuck my head down, making sure the humans can't see me from inside the car, and hope with all my might that this car is going to the same place Carter's car went.

I hold tight to the bike, wishing for a blanket or a cluster of leaves to make the pedal a more comfortable seat. We have soft ropes and blankets and dirt mounds in the Monkey Pit, but it's starting to seem like humans trade comfort for a little

bit more variety in their food. I release a sweet-scented burp and think about doughnuts. Oh, doughnuts.

As the car carrying my bike gains speed, the strength of the wind forces the bird to flutter off my tiara and fly up into the sky. "You're crazy, monkey!" she shouts.

That's the last thing I hear as my car zooms through the human gate and away from the zoo.

A Bath Fit for a Monkey

It pains me to say it, but that chirping bird was right.

I was crazy to do this.

My hands are numb from holding on to this bike. My fur is filthy. I'll bet my tiara is dingy and dull. And Carter's backpack? I don't even want to think about it.

Little droplets of water and mud keep flying up from the road, reminding me of just one of the reasons my mom is going to scold me. This mud is going to take years to lick and pick clean. It feels like the car has been rolling forever, but I bet a regular lunch session usually lasts longer than this car ride. I'm simply very uncomfortable.

ZuZu and Timothy are probably just finishing up their lunch now, licking their fingers clean of apples and bread. Oh, and is it honey day? *Bananas!* If I missed honey day, I'll be so mad!

I can't think about honey day. I can't think about ZuZu, or Timothy, or my special branch in the tickling tree that's been rubbed soft from years of jumping and scratching at it. I need to focus on hanging on to this bike perch. Carter will know what to do when I find him in the city. He'll be so grateful that I've brought him his backpack that he'll probably take me to get ZuZu some banana ice cream and bring me to his school for show-and-tell. I smile a little, thinking about how much fun we're going to have.

This is so much better than sitting in the Monkey Pit, watching people walk by. I don't mean *this* exactly—the wet bike pedal I've decided to take for a ride is probably the worst part of this human world. But this adventure, this *risk*... *"Ooh, ooh!"* Thinking about everything I'm going to see and do, I can't stop myself from howling into the wind.

Suddenly, the car slows, then stops. I cast a

quick glance behind me and notice another car coming closer to the back of my car. *"Eeee!"* It's going to hit me. The car is going to *hit me.*

But then it stops.

I'm alive!

I glance into the inside of the car behind me, the one that almost crushed me into monkey mush, and see a human man staring back at me. He shakes his head and wipes at his eyes. He looks sleepy. I wave to him and blow a raspberry kiss— that's what my mom does when I'm tired, and it always makes me giggle.

Then the car with my bike on it starts to roll forward again, and I lose sight of the man in the car behind me. I'm starting to get really uncomfortable. The bike pedal is digging a little hole in my back fur that is not supposed to be there. The mud from the road is drying up, leaving my fluffy hair clumped and patchy. I bet I look like a squirrel after they fall into the monkey stream. They always look so funny, wet squirrels. It's like all the hair on their tails fell off or something. Serves them right for crashing our pad. They have their own area of the zoo—why do they always come in and steal *our* food?

The next time the car stops, I decide it's time to make a break for it. There are so many cars surrounding us now, and a lot of buildings and people. Everything feels so different from the fields and roads that we'd past while driving away from the zoo. I think we must be in the city. The Human City.

All I need to do now is find Carter. I loosen my fingers and toes from their hold on the bike and slide off the back of the car. I hop away from the car just as it rolls forward again, and I dash between two other cars that are sitting, unmoving, on the side of the road.

My tummy is aching again—maybe it's still from the doughnuts—and I can't stop thinking about how nice a proper lunch would be right about now. But I realize no one is going to serve me, looking like I do. My mom would call me grubby. I need to wash up before I sit down for a meal.

I'm sure the humans must have the same rules. No one wants to eat with a monkey that stinks and has a tarnished tiara.

I look around, searching for a good place for washing. But I can't see anything at all, since I'm absolutely overwhelmed by just how many *people* there are. And if I thought the zoo had a lot of buildings and benches and *stuff*, well, the Human City is unbelievable. How am I ever going to find Carter? Where will I even start?

Before I begin to panic, I spot a little bath just a few steps away in a small grassy space. Oh, and look, an agility course!

I creep toward the bath slowly, trying to hide so no one can see my matted fur. The bath is really cool. It's small—more appropriately sized for a small monkey to sit in than for a human child—and it has a neat handle thing that you turn to make the water come out.

I place Carter's backpack carefully on the ground next to the bath, then climb up and into the bowl. When I twist the handle, a fountain of water comes shooting out, straight into the side of my belly. I shimmy and spin, letting the water run across my whole body while picking at the clumps of mud to loosen them.

I can feel my fur rinsing clean as I wash, and I know I'm going to look absolutely *fine* when I finish my bath. We need to get one of these little baths in the Monkey Pit—the pond is nice, but you have to splash yourself. This stream of water spurting from the bath is so convenient.

When I notice two small people standing next to me, mouths open, I realize I've been a little greedy about my time in the bath. I grin at the kids, and . . .

Shake!

Shake!

Shake!

"*Ayee!*" I screech happily as the water flies off my body and I feel my fur fluff up. Oh boy, does it feel fantastic to be fresh and clean and sparkly!

But instead of giving me a high five or a tail thump the way ZuZu would to celebrate the end of a bath, the children run, screaming, "There's a monkey in the drinking fountain!" I pull my tiara off my head and glance into its shiny surface, searching for my reflection.

I look pretty—extra fluffy, even! I'm not sure what they're so freaked out about, but if this is what people in the city act like when they see monkeys, I prefer the people at the zoo.

Monkey Jokes

"Knock, knock."

"Who's there?" I grumble.

"You!"

"You who?" My eyes are drooping...

"Yoo-hoo to you too!" For the past hour, I've been curled up at the top of a tree in the park, listening to the most unfunny chipmunk crack jokes. It's as though the chipmunk has been saving up all his worst jokes for the day some poor, unsuspecting monkey would just miraculously appear in the Human City.

That poor monkey is me.

"Knock, knock."

I lean back and rest my head on Carter's backpack. It actually makes a nice pillow, and I can feel my eyes fluttering closed. "Who's there?"

"Albee!"

"Albee who?" Chipmunks are worse than squirrels. That's for sure.

"Albee a monkey!" The chipmunk chatters out a laugh. "Get it? *I'll* be a monkey! But I'm not a monkey, I'm a chipmunk."

"No kidding," I mutter. I think I'd rather spend the afternoon watching Timothy throw his lunch. This chipmunk is really getting to me. And he's been absolutely no help in my quest to find Carter.

The chipmunk runs up and down the tree trunk, squeaking, "No kidding! No kidding!" I have got to get away from this maniac.

"Listen," I say seriously. I'm a monkey on the run with a lost backpack and need to find my friend. "You said you knew Carter."

"Carter the monkey?"

I stare at the chipmunk and he flicks his tail nervously. Just being near this nut is making me twitch. "No . . . Carter the boy. *I'm* a monkey." This seems rather obvious, but I wonder if maybe ol' Chippy here has a hair or two loose.

"Ohhhh!" The chipmunk scrambles on the branch, scattering bark and sending it floating down to the grass below. "I thought you were looking for Carter the *monkey*." The chipmunk lets out this high-pitched trilling noise and looks at me. "Because Carter the *monkey* is right here." He points at me.

"No, I'm Willa," I explain. Again.

"*Aha!*" The chipmunk says. "I'm Willa too."

"No, you're a chipmunk."

"Yes, a chipmunk named Willa. And we are looking for a boy named Monkey, correct?"

I don't think monkeys and chipmunks are meant to hang out. I'm starting to think we might speak different languages. "Listen, chipmunk—"

"Call me Willa," the chipmunk insists, cutting me off. "Willa the chipmunkey."

"Your name is not Willa," I declare. "You're only saying that because that's my name."

"Yes. It's a good name. I'll take it."

"You can't take my name!" I shout, then realize how loud I'm speaking. There is really no need to be getting so angry at this ridiculous chipmunk. I just need to say good-bye, and get back on my way. "If you can't help me, I'm leaving. I need to find Carter to bring him his backpack. He rides in a blue car, he likes ice cream from Frank's, and he goes to school at a place called Lakeside Elementary."

The chipmunk nods seriously. "I know about all of those places."

"You do?" I'm suspicious, but hopeful.

"I'll tell you what . . . let's cuddle and nap, then I'll take you there."

"Cuddle?"

"You look so soft. I like to cuddle." This chipmunk is quickly becoming the strangest friend I've ever had. He might even be weirder than Sloth, the giant monkey who sits alone all day just shouting things at the humans and trying to pelt them with apples and bugs. "Can we take a quick snooze, and then be off on our Carter-hunting mission?"

I can feel my eyes drooping, and wonder if maybe a nap is a good idea. It's been a really busy day, and this tree is awfully comfortable. There's a big flat spot where all the branches meet and form a sort of hole that I can curl up inside. I can look for food and Carter when I wake up, right? "I'm willing to nap, but you have to promise me . . . no more jokes. Also, I won't agree to cuddle," I tell the chipmunk, already slipping into a sleepy trance.

"Can I just hold your tail then? Like a lovey?" The chipmunk already has my tail in his hands and has draped it up and over his neck like a scarf. "Us Willas need to stick together, you know?"

Team Willa

When I wake up, I'm surrounded by nuts. My body is covered in piles of acorns and pinecones, but there are also a whole bunch of chipmunks keeping a watchful eye on me. I can't figure out which chipmunk I'd been talking to before my nap, since they all sort of look the same.

It seems like all chipmunks are small and runty and strange.

When they realize my eyes are open, all the chipmunks start singing to me. They're singing "Happy Birthday"—off-key. "Happy birthday to you, happy birthday to you, you look like a monkey, and you smell like one too!"

"Hey! It's not my birthday!" I say, wiping the sleepiness from my eyes.

"Yes it is," a chipmunk squeaks. The same chipmunk I'd been dealing with earlier? No clue. "You're ten today."

"Willa made you a mud cake, but we ate it while you were sleeping," another chipmunk declares. They all even sound the same! *Ugh*, I guess we're still doing this same-name thing.

I can't help but smile—when they're not telling jokes, chipmunks are pretty funny, really. It's not my birthday, but I guess I'll play along. It's always nice to be the center of attention. "Well, thanks, Willa," I say, lifting my tiara. "I do love cake."

"You're welcome," echoes an entire chorus of chipmunks.

"Wait . . . ," I ask, confused. "Which of you said your name is Willa?"

"Me!" All of the chipmunks answer together.

"So what you're saying is that every one of you is named Willa? Just like me?"

"Except me!" A little chipmunk that has been hiding in Carter's backpack pipes up. "My name is

Carter." I'm pretty sure *this* is the chipmunk I'd met earlier. The jokester. He had apparently changed his name from Willa to Carter. *Great.*

I groan. "Well, then." I scratch at a rough spot on my foot. All the chipmunks follow suit, except Carter the chipmunk, who is now sitting on my shoulder nuzzling against my cheek fluff. "I guess this means all of you are coming along to help me find Carter?"

"Carter is right here," announces the little chipmunk on my shoulder.

"Yes," I nod. "I see that. I need to find Carter the boy." It's very obvious that there will be no escaping these chipmunks, so I'd better get used to the idea of a team of fake Willas (and one fake Carter) assisting me in my search.

My little followers are actually sort of comforting, since I'm starting to feel a little homesick. I've never gone this long without Mom or ZuZu or Timothy or Delilah Delilah the Third or the other monkeys in the Pit. I guess chipmunks are a little bit like small monkeys. I can pretend, anyway. "Do you think maybe we could start our search for Carter at Frank's? I'm starving."

"You're hungry?" one of the chipmunks cries.

"Why didn't you say something sooner? We've got a guy who can take care of that for you."

"You have a zookeeper?" *Do chipmunks get meal delivery, just like monkeys?* I wonder.

"Zookeeper?" One chipmunk scoffs. "No way. We've got Frank!"

Okay, now we were onto something. We are finally going to follow one of my leads—hopefully, we'll find Carter at Frank's! "Can you take me there?" I ask reluctantly, since I am still a little hesitant to rely on these odd chipmunks for anything. "Can we go there now?"

But the chipmunks don't answer, since they're suddenly totally obsessed with stuffing the acorns and pinecones that are piled on my body into Carter's backpack. When every last nut and cone is stuffed inside, the little chipmunk—the one who is now calling himself Carter—hops inside the pack and gets comfy on top of the pile.

I sigh. Then I zip the compartment shut carefully, leaving a peek hole for the little chipmunk's head, and flip the whole heavy pack onto my back. Then I scurry down the tree to follow a parade of silly chipmunks.

Mice and Beans

Frank's is *not* what I expected.

First of all, Frank is a rat. A fat, filthy insect-ridden rat. And these aren't the kind of insects that look tasty; they just look dirty and spicy.

Also, there are no humans at Frank's and there probably never will be. My first clue that this place isn't fit for people came when we had to crawl through the back door of a shop and scamper between two giant waste containers to enter—one of the chipmunks called it an alley. So far, I'm not really an alley fan. I guess I didn't need to bathe to dine at Frank's—the place is a dump.

I sashay delicately between bones and piles of rotting fruit, keeping a close eye on the path in front of me in order to avoid stepping in something gross. There is no way that this is the place Carter's grandma takes him for their special treats after school.

"What can I do for you today, kids?" Frank sneers at us, his milky yellow eyes crusted over with some sort of rat pus. Would it be polite to let Frank know about the cute bath I found, just across the street in the park? I mean, if you're going to serve food, the least you can do is clean up just a touch. Our human, Emily, always smells really nice—like apples and milk—when she brings our meal delivery to the Pit.

"Monkey needs a snack," one of the chipmunks explains.

"You got anything for me?" Frank turns his oozy eyes on me and I look at the floor. "You! If you want to eat, you gotta give ol' Frank something in return."

"We'll work it out—what's on your menu today?" The same chipmunk speaks again. The rest of them stand there in a cluster, all huddled together with their tails pointing to the sky.

"I'd like something called ice cream," I say hopefully. "Banana?"

Frank laughs. "I'd like ice cream too. What I've got is this—" He gestures to a pile of scraps on the ground. The only things I can identify are an old apple core, the crust of bread, a rotting pile of beans, and some sort of meat. The meat has a bite out of it. *Ew.*

"I don't eat crust," I say haughtily. I mean, come on, who likes *crust*...for real? "And that apple is already eaten. Do you have any fresh food? I'd be okay with a banana, or maybe some apples drizzled with honey?"

Frank's teeth chatter when he laughs. I don't like this rat at all. "Well, well, aren't you a princess."

"Yes. I am." How does he know Princess is my proper first name?

"I'm afraid that if you want to eat at Frank's, you take what I've got. And today, what I've got is this." He pokes his snout into the pile of rotting food, making it even less appetizing than it had been a few moments before. I think a little snot may have run out of his nostril and onto the piles of beans.

I look around at the inquisitive chipmunk faces, still all squished together in a clump of chipmunkiness. They are obviously watching me carefully to see how I'm going to respond. But it's an easy decision—I wouldn't eat this food if it were delivered to the Monkey Pit, and I'm surely not going to eat it here. "No, thank you." I turn up my nose at the pile of filth and turn to leave.

"I need your payment," Frank demands.

"But I didn't eat anything," I protest.

"You pay to visit Frank's," the rat insists merrily. "If you don't like my menu, that's your problem. But I've got a limit to how many customers I can have in here at any one time, and you and your posse have been taking up all the space. Tough tootsies that you don't want to eat—you still owe me for my time."

I can't believe this guy—who does he think he is? I look at the chipmunks hopefully. Didn't one of them say something about working it out? "Can you guys help?" Not a single chipmunk says anything now.

"You better pay up," Frank says, snorting his filthy breath in my direction.

I try pleading with the chipmunks. "I thought you said you'd work it out?"

I can hear little Carter the chipmunk (or whatever his real name is), still in the backpack on my back, squeaking fearfully. "Chipmunks like to tell jokes—we were teasing and doing a truth stretch," he whispers in my ear. "In case you haven't noticed."

Frank lumbers toward me, his glistening fangs flashing. "That's a pretty snazzy backpack you've got there," he taunts. "How about we work out a trade? That's the perfect payment."

"You want me to give you this backpack?" I ask, shocked. "But it's not even my backpack. It belongs to a little boy."

Frank sighs. "Oh ho, that's my favorite kind of prize . . . a stolen treasure."

"It's not stolen!" I cry. "I'm trying to bring it back to him."

"Well, that's not gonna happen." Frank crowds toward me, his claws and teeth suddenly much bigger than they'd appeared mere moments before.

When I check to see who has my back, I see that the chipmunks are all tiptoeing toward the door in unison. Sneaking away. I'm going to be left all alone, with only poor Carter the chipmunk, who is zipped inside the backpack's pocket.

Frank puckers his filmy rat lips before lunging at me. "I know it's not going to happen. Because that backpack? It's mine now."

Chipmunk Chatter

Just as Frank's oozing teeth lurch at me, I hear *chitter, chatter,* and a tinny *bang* behind me. The chipmunks—who I thought were long gone, escaped to the safety of their tree—have piled atop one another to build a little tower of chipmunks. They're tall enough to knock an empty can off the top of a garbage container in the alley. The noise rings out, clattering loudly, and Frank turns away from me for just an instant.

In that instant, I run. Monkeys are fast, and it just so happens that monkeys being chased by slimy rats are even faster. Also handy? I can jump.

Even with the weight of the nut- and chipmunk-filled backpack on my shoulders, I am able to leap up on top of a garbage can, then hop to a ladder on the side of a building.

I fly up the ladder all the way to the roof. Only then do I look down to see that Frank is stuck on the ground—the ladder is too high for him to reach with his shifty little claws. I lift my arm in the air to do a fist-pump celebration. I'm hopping and dancing and celebrating my escape when I hear a soft whimper behind me. Carter the chipmunk. I forgot I have a tiny passenger.

"Are you okay?" I ask. "Wasn't that fun?"

"I guess," Carter the chipmunk whines. "But where is my family?"

I glance off the side of the building and see a line of chipmunks running across the street, headed for the park. They're actually pretty cute when they zoom like that. "They're safe," I assure the little chipmunk. "And thanks to them, so are we. Is Frank always scary like that?"

"Pretty much, yeah."

"Um, Carter? Why do you eat there?"

"Oh, we don't." The chipmunk mumbles in my ear. I can hear him burrowing, and I wonder if he's trying to get out of the backpack. "We eat the nuts and berries we find in the park or at humans' houses. Frank's is more of a special-occasion establishment."

"How do you mean?" I reach around to take the backpack off my back and open the zipper compartment to let the little chipmunk out. From up here on top of the building, we have nice views of the park across the street and lots of cars down below us. I can see kids playing and running and jumping, and it makes me wonder what ZuZu is up to. He's probably starting to get ready for dinner—the thought makes my stomach rumble. I'm so hungry I would almost be willing to give up my tiara if Emily would just *appear* right at this moment.

"Most of the animals around here find their own food. We hunt and gather and visit human yards to eat seeds."

"Do humans eat seeds?" I ask curiously. My little friend has settled onto his haunches at my side and is pulling acorns out of the backpack to stack them in little piles on the roof. It reminds me of how Timothy sometimes stacks bits of leftover food and dirt alongside his body to throw at other monkeys. I hope Carter isn't planning to throw his acorns my way. They look a lot harder than grapes.

I watch the little chipmunk working, and I can't even believe how busy he is. As soon as he gets one pile made, he starts to move all the acorns to build a new pile. I'm being surrounded by acorn clusters. He takes a quick break to answer me. "Humans must *love* seeds. After their meals, they leave these nice little plates and boxes of leftover seeds and nuts out in their backyards for us. We call it a backyard buffet. The birds always call the buffets *bird feeders*, but that's just because they're really self-centered. They aren't very good at sharing, so we usually have to push them out of the way when we get there."

"Our zookeeper leaves food out for us. She's a human too. Emily is really nice. She lives at the zoo." At least, I always thought she did. But maybe she lives with Carter, here in the Human City? No way. That's too weird to think about. Emily *definitely* lives at the zoo.

"Do *you* live at the zoo?" Carter looks surprised. "How did you get out?"

"I just jumped," I say simply. "My friend ZuZu distracted the Elders and I went for it."

"So you've never been to the city before?" Carter stops scurrying for a second to ask, "Do you miss the other monkeys, Willa?"

Even though it's only been half a day that I've been away from the Monkey Pit, it feels like months. I miss my friends like crazy, and I'm starting to wonder if my mom is worried about me. I don't want her to worry—she should be worrying about whether Timothy will accidentally hit a human with a grape bomb, not about whether or not I'm safe. "Yes, I really miss them."

I also miss my treasures, but I don't say that.

"Do you think you'll ever go back for a visit?"

"For a visit?" I'm surprised at this question. "It's where I live—I'm going back forever, just as soon as I return Carter's backpack to him."

Carter the chipmunk rubs his hands together. "How are you going to get back to the zoo?"

I hadn't thought that far. . . . "Ride a car, I guess?"

"Oh."

The chipmunk won't look at me, and it's making me nervous. "What's wrong with taking a car?"

"It's just . . ." He starts scurrying again. "It's just

that humans don't welcome most animals in their cars or their houses or their restaurants or anywhere, really. One time, one of my friends tried to go into a restaurant and she was chased out of there with a broom and a can of something really stinky. She smelled worse than a rat and her backside was all scratched up from the broom."

"What did she do to make the humans so angry?" I ask. "Did she steal their food?"

"Nothing. I guess humans just don't like animals that much. Except for this one animal they do seem to like snuggling with—these foul creatures with bad breath and big teeth." Carter shudders. "Humans call them dogs."

I remember sitting in the tickling tree just this morning, when ZuZu told me about dogs—the cleaning animals. I definitely wouldn't want to get licked clean by something with big teeth and bad breath! Carter chews at a pinecone and keeps talking while I imagine what dogs might look like— all I can picture are alligators with fur. *Yick!* "I guess it's just that humans don't like to share their space. They put food out in their backyards, but they don't really like to see us or know we're eating off their plate."

I don't believe that. I think about all the humans that visit the zoo every day—they love animals, right? But maybe that's because we're tucked away inside our cages, fenced in. I think back to the humans who stared at me as I ran through the zoo earlier today—they looked surprised and a little scared to see me out of the Pit. Maybe this chipmunk is right.

Well, there's only one way to find out. Carter is out there, somewhere in the human world, and I am going to have to risk mingling with the humans if I want to have any hope of finding him.

The Chase

It's been decided. I will have a companion in my quest for Carter the boy. Carter the chipmunk is determined to come with me as my Human City tour guide, and I guess I'm happy to have the help—even if chipmunks are too silly to be truly helpful.

After another fifteen minutes on the roof, I finally convince my chipmunk tagalong to leave his piles of acorns behind. If I have to tote a chipmunk in the pack on my back, I don't want to have to carry his snacks all around the city too. They're heavy!

"So, where should we start?" Carter the chipmunk asks, stuffing a few final acorns into his cheeks. It seems impossible that anything else could fit in his tiny little mouth, but I think he has at least ten acorns saved in there for later. His cheeks look stretched, and you can see the outline of the nuts under the skin. *Ouch.* "What do you want to see first?"

"Well, I guess we should try to find Lakeside Elementary or Frank's—the ice-cream place—or maybe the library? Those are all the places Carter told me about when we were talking this morning, so let's start with one of those." I open the back-pack's compartment and point to show the chipmunk that he needs to crawl in. When he's all settled, I zip up the sides so he won't tumble out and prepare to pick it up again. "Can you lead me there?"

"Absolutely, Willa. You can trust me."

I roll my eyes. I don't trust Carter, but I have no choice but to follow his lead. "Is your name really Carter?" I ask, squinting my eyes at him as I push my lips into a full pucker to show that he can't fool me. "I want the truth, chipmunk. No more jokes."

Carter the chipmunk tucks his head down

against the top of the backpack and lays his cute chubby cheeks on his teensy-weensy hands. "I like when you call me Carter," he peeps out, eventually. "I know he's your friend, and I want to be your friend."

I blow my cheeks out and then release the air in a noisy raspberry. "You *are* my friend! That's why I want to know your real name."

"Chipmunks don't really have names. We just say 'Hey!' and 'You!' and that works well enough." He chatters around the lumps of acorns that stuff his cheeks. "I have an idea. . . . How about you call me Chipmunkey? It really works, since today I'm just as much a monkey as I am a chipmunk. Two adventurers, out on a quest, doing monkey things."

I pull the backpack over my shoulders and mutter, "We're not the same, and you're *not* a monkey. But I'll call you Chipmunkey. That's kind of cute."

"Really?" Chipmunkey chatters. "So we're buddies, Willa?"

"Yep, buddies." Then I bound down the ladder and peek into the street. I guess this is it. It's time to make a break for it, back into the Human City to find Carter. I step gingerly away from the building and dart into the street. I instantly regret it. A car screams at me and I squeal.

"Hey, Willa? You should stay on the sidewalk. That's where people are walking—the street is just for cars."

"Okay," I say, still shaking from the sound of that car's horrible scream. "Got it. Sidewalk."

I scuttle back to the sidewalk, walking on just two feet so as to call as little attention to myself as possible. If I walk like a human, maybe no one will notice me. But I guess these people aren't used to seeing a monkey with a chipmunk on her back every day, because I'm obviously very noticeable. Perhaps it's my tiara.

"Look! A monkey!" someone shouts from an open shop window. "A monkey with a crown. *Aw!*"

I touch my tiara delicately, proud that they noticed its beauty. "Actually, it's a tiara," I explain, hopping excitedly. "I also have an earring and a plastic fork and a barrette and a baseball cap—"

I'm still chattering happily when someone right next to me yells, "The monkey's freaking out! Someone get it!"

"I'm not freaking out," I protest, stepping away from the human. I start waving my arms in the air

to show them that I'm just being nice and would be more than happy to give someone a hug to show them that I'm friendly, but this seems to alarm the humans even more. "I just wanted to tell you about my treasures!" I exclaim, backing away. I push a loud breath out from between my lips—this is unbelievable!

"Get it before it attacks someone!" A guy with a broom shouts. He stalks toward me and is quickly joined by a woman holding a long stick with wiggly strings on the end—it looks like a broom with hair.

"Willa! Look out! A broom! And a mop!" Chipmunkey doesn't need to tell me—I saw them and immediately think about Chipmunkey's friend, the one who was *attacked* by a broom. Why are they out to get me? Why are they chasing me? I'm freshly bathed, I'm being overly friendly, and I'm not even taking anyone's food.

This is *not* how things work at the zoo! I can only guess that they must want my tiara—I'll bet they know I took it from the ledge, and now the humans want it back. But the tiara is mine, and I don't want to get hit by a broom. The bristles of the broom look harsh and pointy, and my backside hurts just looking at them. So I run—again. I run like my life depends on it, which I guess it sort of does.

I put my hands on the ground and use all my power to push through the crowds of people. I dash along the sidewalk and the crowds magically part as I approach, making space for me to pass. It's like they *want* me to get away. Chipmunkey is both cheering and whimpering at the same time.

There is suddenly a cluster of birds around me, fluttering and flapping in the annoying way that birds do. I hear one of them say, "You'd better run, monkey!"

"Thanks," I mutter, still running at full speed. "I was thinking I should sit down and have a little snack." *Birds.* They think they're so smart. As if I don't *know* I'm being chased.

We run past kids riding in rolling carts—which are called strollers, Chipmunkey told me when we were sitting up on the roof. The kids point and laugh and shout happily when they see me. Human kids seem to like animals—it must just be the Elders that don't want to play with us outside zoo walls.

I dash by a store that has fruit piled high in

baskets. Then I scurry along a low wall that divides the sidewalk from a cluster of outdoor tables where people are sitting, eating. As I run past, I smell warm bread and sweet apple slices and lettuce and other wonderful delights on the tables. I can't help myself . . . I take a peek over my shoulder to make sure no one is right behind me, then hop over to a table. I grab a piece of bread with my lips and hold it tight as I dart off again. Someone screams, but I focus on Chipmunkey's *yahoo*ing and chuckling behind me instead.

The bread tastes like honey and home as I stuff it into my mouth, and it makes me long for the Monkey Pit. I don't like stealing food, and I don't like people chasing me. It feels like I've done something *wrong*, when really I'm just trying to do something *right*! I just want to bring Carter his backpack—why is everyone so upset that I'm here? I want to help!

But now is not the time to think about this, since I still have a group of noisy people in hot pursuit behind me, and I need to get somewhere safe. When I peek back, I notice that one of the humans is holding an umbrella. It's not even raining! What are they going to do with that umbrella?

Up ahead, I can see a lake. And there, on the side of the lake, are a bunch of little boats just waiting for someone to ride in them. They look like the little boat Emily put in our stream at the beginning of the summer. She had to take it away after Timothy got his leg stuck under it one morning. He made such a stink about it that Emily took it out of the Pit that very day. It was a bummer.

My feet have never moved so fast in my life. I'm so close to the lake I can smell the wetness and the weeds, both of which make my stomach curl. These humans don't seem to respect a monkey's need to eat her bread in comfort and calm. Oh, what I'd give for a quick rest in the tickling tree right about now.

I can still hear the crowds of humans behind me, but their voices are farther away now—too far to catch me.

With one final glance over my shoulder, I leap from the shore into a boat and feel the sloshing of the water beneath the floor under my feet. "Chipmunkey, here we go!"

Float, Boat, Float

It seems that the boat is broken.

When I first jumped aboard it swayed from side to side, but now it's not moving anywhere, except back and forth in exactly the same place. I've been rocking and shuffling my feet and hopping up and down, but this boat isn't sailing away. It's stuck.

The humans, with their brooms and mops and umbrellas, are getting closer by the second and I'm just sitting here like Timothy was that morning his leg got stuck, waiting for them. Chipmunkey is picking at one of the acorns from his cheek.

He's making a *peck-peck*ing sound and doesn't seem at all concerned that we're in a boat that's going nowhere. It's like the acorn is the only thing he can think about. Oh, chipmunks.

"Do you know anything about boats?" I ask Chipmunkey hopefully, pulling off my backpack and setting it on the floor so Chipmunkey can get out. I climb up on the front of the boat and peer out across the water.

He's still crunching away, but looks up briefly to answer. "Nope."

I pull at my ears and twitch my tail. "You do, don't you? Are you just trying to be silly?"

Chipmunkey sets the acorn aside and scampers to the front of the boat to stand beside me. "Knock, knock..."

"I don't want to know who's there, Chipmunkey. I want to know how to drive this boat!"

"Okay, okay," Chipmunkey says, and sighs. "Here's the thing: I do know something about *this* boat, but not boats in general."

"How can we make this boat go?" I prod. "We need to get out of here now."

"There's a rope hooked around a post onshore. We're all tied up."

I hop over to the back of the boat—Chipmunkey's right. There's a rope looped around a post right onshore. All I need to do is hop out of the boat, unhook the loop, and jump back into the boat before it floats away. Easy-peasy.

I climb over the edge of the boat and start to tug at the rope. Chipmunkey relaxes back on one of the boat's benches and works at cracking into his acorn. My fingers are a little too small for this to be a simple job, but I'm determined.

"Can I finish my joke now?" Chipmunkey begs.

I can hear the roar of the humans getting closer. They sound crabby, like the Human Elders that visit the zoo right before lunchtime. Just one more tug, then . . . *pop!* The rope is off the post and the boat is floating free.

I bend my legs and prepare to pounce back into the boat, but within an instant the boat has blown away from shore, and the jump is impossibly far. I need to land a jump almost twice the distance of the tickling tree to the ledge. There's no way I can make it! The boat holding Chipmunkey and Carter's backpack is floating away without me.

"Willa!" Chipmunkey has just realized what's happening and is running frantically from side to side in the boat. He is so tiny that the boat barely even moves as he scampers back and forth. "Willa! I'm sorry I was telling another knock-knock joke! I'm afraid of the water. I'm not joking about this—I'm not! I'm really, really afraid of the water!"

I want to tell the little chipmunk not to panic, but I'm really scared. I'm the one that put him in the boat, and I need to figure out how to get him back to shore. But I don't swim and I can't jump that far, and I see now that the humans are almost to the lake. What I need is a plan—

I wish ZuZu were here. He'd come up with something clever!

The boat is floating farther and farther out into the lake, carried away by the waves and wind. Zuzu's not here—and I need to act. About forty hops away, I can see a tree with long branches that sway down over the water, just past the boat. I tense the muscles in my legs and bound forward along the ground, but I quickly realize running will take too long. I climb up into a tree and swing from one branch to another, following the boat as it bobs gently in the water.

I hop from branch to branch, high up in the treetops, and try to remember all of my lessons from last year. I am a great climber and jumper, but I've never been a super swinger. I got a "Needs Improvement" during that unit at school. I'm going to have to improve *today*. I reach the tree with dangling branches and slip down one of its arms until I'm close to the water, just inches off the lake's surface. The boat is getting closer and will pass me in a moment.

"Chipmunkey, climb in the backpack!" I instruct. He hesitates, but then scrambles in. The backpack is leaning against one of the benches, and I know this is my only chance. "Tuck down deep into the pocket and hang on, little chipmunk!" He burrows his body deep into the pocket, tucking in close to Carter's gemstone treasure.

Just as the boat passes beneath my tree, I wrap my legs around the dangling tree branch and let my body drape down toward the water. My fingers touch the wet surface, then the edge of the boat bumps against my hands.

I reach in and—*snap!*—grab the backpack. I hold it tightly with one hand, careful to keep it upright, and use my other hand and my two feet to scoot back up the dangling branch. When I get to a place I can sit down safely, I zip up the backpack, leaving only a tiny head hole for Chipmunkey to peek out of. Then I sling the backpack on my back and fly through the trees.

I see the group of angry humans running up to the lakeshore—they can't see me up in the trees. I can't help but smile when I see them climb into boats to go out into the lake. They think Chipmunkey and I are still in the empty boat. ZuZu would be really proud—I'm not so bad at this whole "plan" thing!

Eyes on the Prizes

The sun is setting over the lake. The world is painted pink and gold and deep blue—it's amazing to see so much of the sky from the tops of the trees outside the zoo. Inside the Monkey Pit, I can only see a little slice of the sky, never the very edges. The edge of the sky is beautiful with colors all mixed and twisted where it meets the trees.

I want to sit and enjoy the view, saving all of this in my memory to share with ZuZu and Timothy when I get home. But I feel nerves bubbling up inside when I realize the darkening sky means the day is almost over and I haven't found Carter.

I know my mom must be really worried. I've never spent a night away from home before, and I have no idea where I'm going to sleep. I hadn't planned this far ahead—I guess I thought it would be a lot easier to find Carter. We would hug, and he'd give me a little prize for returning his back-pack. Then he'd put the pack on his back to carry me home to the zoo, the way I've been carrying Chipmunkey all day.

But that hadn't happened. Instead, I am all alone with a silly chipmunk and a still-hungry stomach, lost in the Human City.

After resting for just a few minutes, I run all the way around the lake, then follow my own scent away from the lake and back into the center of the city. The streets are less crowded now, and I think I've figured out how to stay hidden behind trash cans and up in trees as I make my way along the sidewalk. I don't want to risk another chase, and I have to find somewhere that looks safe to spend the night.

"How about there?" Chipmunkey is pointing at a dingy, dark-looking space between two build-ings. I shiver, thinking about our run-in with Frank the rat earlier in the day.

"No way," I grumble. I don't want to admit that I am set on finding somewhere with a blanket or at least a roof over my head. Not that I'm spoiled or anything, but the zoo gives us pretty sweet sleeping quarters. My family's den is really cozy and warm—is that too much luxury to expect here in the Human City?

"There?" Chipmunkey suggests, sticking his little paw out toward a chilly-looking gray building at the top of some hard steps. There are people coming out of the building and none of them are smiling. It can't be a very friendly place if everyone looks so unhappy. So I keep scrambling along, peeking quietly into doors of restaurants and cafés filled with humans eating scrumptious meals on comfy chairs.

"There! A store!" Chipmunkey shouts suddenly, and I know instantly which place he's talking about. Across the street, there's a big, bright building with windows for walls. This "store" thing looks like a great sleeping den. Through the windows, I can see all kinds of wonders . . . beautiful dresses, colorful purses, racks filled with scarves and hats and *treasures*!

I smell the delicious aroma of food wafting out

the doors of this store, and I can barely even contain myself. I make a run for it, dodging into a spinning door that moves on its own. The door spits me out on the inside of the building and I take it all in. The smells are magical. I want to run and dance and shout happily, but I know I need to stay hidden, so I quickly duck into a corner, behind a rack of dresses that no one is wearing.

Chipmunkey is sucking in all the scents too. I can hear him snorting with his tiny little nose, right into my ear, and I realize I can probably let him out of the backpack now. His tiny snuffling is sort of tickly, and I'm afraid it's going to make me giggle.

I open the backpack's zipper to release him. He runs excitedly, spinning in circles. Then he settles back on his haunches and spits an acorn out of his cheek to start in on another meal. I don't understand how this guy is still so small—he's *always* eating!

I slink under a rack of human clothes and peek out into the store. My tail instantly pokes up into the rack of clothing to rub against the soft fabrics—I can't control it. I'm just too excited. These human treasures feel so soft and silky on my fur, and I could spend the whole day just snuggling against the dresses. I spot miles of pink loveliness and think of my mom. She would be happy here; I'm just sure of it.

There are people everywhere, and I can't figure out how my pal and I are ever going to avoid being noticed. It seems like most people are sticking to a little trail that runs down the center of the room. This must be the sidewalk, since it's where all the people are walking. I wonder, if we move along the walls, will anyone be able to see us?

It's worth the risk, since I absolutely *need* to explore this human wonderland. My nose is twitching excitedly at the sweet scents coming from *somewhere*, and I want to hop and shout, "*Where* is that *food*?" But I keep my mouth zipped, since it's sometimes hard to keep my voice at the right volume level. I've already discovered that monkey shouts scare humans when we're outside the zoo, and I don't want anyone to know I'm here. I just need a little snack and a snooze and then we can go back outside in the morning to look for Carter again.

Chipmunkey stuffs the half-eaten acorn back inside his cheek and follows me along the wall of the store. We're both making ourselves as small as possible, tiptoeing under racks of clothes and hanging hats and bags. Suddenly, an impossibly loud voice comes out of the walls: "Shoppers, Ludlow's will be closing in five minutes. Please complete your purchases and have a pleasant evening."

My head whips around, trying to figure out where the voice came from. It sounded like a human, but I could have sworn it was the wall talking. But then I stop, thinking about what the voice had said—the store is closing! If that means the same thing here as it does at the zoo, then the humans will all go somewhere else, and Chipmunkey and I will be free to explore! There are no fences holding us back, no humans chasing us, and no one to tell us where we can and can't go or what we can and can't touch. It's like paradise. Treasure land!

I already have my eye on a brilliant fuzzy yellow scarf that would make my fur feel so good . . . I can't wait to wrap it around my neck and snuggle in for the night! *There will be time to find Carter in the morning,* I promise myself. *A monkey needs to relax, right?*

House of Paint and Treasures

"You look gorgeous!" I purr while holding four different color sticks, one in each of my hands and feet. I guess the color sticks are called "lipstick"—at least, that's what Chipmunkey told me—but I'm never sure if he's being funny or serious. Lipstick doesn't seem like a very glamorous name for such a fancy thing, so I will call them color sticks, since that's what they look like to me. "Should we try pink next?"

Chipmunkey and I have found the most marvelous place. After all the humans left the store, we decided to seek out the source of the sweet food smells. It turned out the aromas were coming from a large room filled with apples and bananas and small carrots and cakes that made me think about doughnuts. We ate until I felt sick, then rested in a room filled with comfy pillows.

When we eventually set out to explore our surroundings, I could hardly believe our luck—we found a big open area filled with little paints and brushes and colors that are meant for us to put on our bodies! Chipmunkey's itty-bitty face is painted a fancy orangey red, and I've covered my lips in a shiny purple gloss. I never would have guessed painting your body in colors could be so fantastically fun.

There are also these cool little mirrors everywhere that you can look into and see yourself. I now know that I do look absolutely lovely in my tiara. And a little color stick makes me look even more beautiful. "Hey!" Chipmunkey calls out from across the store. "Come and have a sniff of this!"

I bound over tables full of color sticks and powders and glosses and find Chipmunkey sitting in the middle of a little circle made of bottles. His nose is poking into one of the bottles and he peeks his head up to mutter, "Vanilla."

My nose is twitching, overwhelmed by scents, but I poke into one of the jars anyway. Each little bottle and jar has its own special smell and every one is more glorious than the next. "This one smells like blueberry!" I cry, and my nose instinctively seeks out the next delicious scent. "And this one reminds me of spring roses blooming in the zoo's gardens! Emily brings them into the Monkey Pit sometimes."

After we sniff every bottle, I lead Chipmunkey to the rack of scarves and purses and necklaces.

Chipmunkey is being so silly, dashing in and out of bags and cases, so I join him. We wrap ourselves in scarves and burrow into things, chasing each other in the biggest game of hide-and-seek ever. I collect more and more treasures as the game goes on, and soon I'm wearing strings of necklaces and scarves and hats and have a purse on each arm. I can't decide what my mom would like best, so I think I better try on absolutely everything.

When we stop to rest (so Chipmunkey can eat another acorn), I realize how sleepy I am. It's been such a grand day, but my stomach hurts thinking about my mom and ZuZu and little Timothy, back at the zoo, worrying about whether I'm safe or not. I pull a scarf up over my head and tell Chipmunkey what I'm thinking about. "I really miss the zoo."

"Wouldn't you like to stay here in the Human City with me forever?" he asks. His little orange-painted face pokes hopefully out of the top of a shiny black purse. "We're having so much fun, and you could live with us in the trees at the park. I'll share my sleep hole!"

"I've had the best day," I admit. "But I miss the other monkeys. I'm getting tired of running and hiding and sneaking around." I feel the softness of the scarf on my neck and rub my lips together, which makes the gloss slip and slide. "There are so many wonderful treasures in the human world—but it's more fun to be able to talk to humans and do tricks for them than it is to slink around, hiding."

I'm surprised to realize this is all true. As much as I love the freedom and wildness of the space outside the zoo's fence—not to mention all the treasures—I want to be somewhere I belong. I want to take Air Acrobatics, and I want Emily to bring me my lunch, and I want to swing with ZuZu on honey day. I tell Chipmunkey all about the funny ideas and plans that ZuZu comes up with to trick other monkeys and our zookeepers. I laugh about Timothy's habit of launching grape missiles at me from high up on our family branch. Finally, I brag about my mom and our teachers and Emily.

I start to feel sad and itchy realizing that I might miss Timothy's first day in Basic Skills—who's going to hug him after he falls the first time? (Because he will definitely fall.) The Human City has a lot of great stuff, but so does the zoo—and even as I snuggle up here, wrapped in soft, scarfy goodness, I miss the Monkey Pit. I miss the humans that like to be near monkeys and not just stinky bad-breathy dogs. I miss home.

"Willa, tomorrow we're going to find Carter. I promise."

Even though I know Chipmunkey can't really make this promise, I want to believe my chipmunk friend. Because I'm ready to go home.

Bus Top

In the morning, I am startled awake by the sound of loud roaring. I peek out of the purse I'm nestled in and see a human man pushing a giant machine across the floor of the store. It makes a horrible sound, and the man is singing loudly over the noise of the machine. He sounds angry, and is wearing these big earmuffs that make him look like, well, a monkey.

I twitch nervously, thinking about the time this lady came into the Monkey Pit with a giant straw that sucked all the water out of our stream. ZuZu and I heard the woman telling Emily a pump broke—something called algae had moved into the water. I don't know what algae are, but I didn't like that they were the reason we lost our cool splashing spot on the hottest days of the summer.

I can hear the machine getting closer, and I cover my ears. I bet that machine has teeth like an alligator—I don't want to find out!

"That's a vacuum cleaner, Willa," Chipmunkey explains, rubbing his eyes with his front feet. "Stay away from them. They're powerful—they like to suck stuff up, including tails and tiaras."

I shudder at the thought, burrowing back into the warmth of my nest to hide from the vacuum man. Then I realize that vacuum cleaner could suck up Carter's backpack! So I sit up quickly again and peek out of my purse to make sure Carter's backpack is still there, sitting on the shelf beside me. It is—and I grin and giggle when I see how nice it looks all dressed up with the feather scarf I'd draped over it right before I fell asleep the night before. It looks like a silly bird backpack.

When I lean over the edge of the shelf we're resting on, I realize that other humans are coming back into the store—the doors must be open! I stretch my arms and yawn, dropping my tiara into place on my head. "We should probably get out of here before someone finds us," I tell the sleepy chipmunk as I put all of the treasures back on their shelves. I wish I could take something for Mom, but I know nothing here belongs to me. "Carter's school is supposed to start today, so if we can figure out where Lakeside Elementary is, we'll definitely be able to give him his backpack."

"Oh, oh! Last night, I thought of something that might be able to help us," Chipmunkey tells me as he climbs inside the backpack again, ready to go for a ride with me. "I went exploring during hide-and-seek and *realized* something. It's a *really* good idea. Take me over there and I'll show you!" Chipmunkey is pointing toward a door with his tiny front feet, so I sweep the backpack up and onto my back and dash off along the wall in the direction he's pointing. I can still hear the roar of the vacuum cleaner and hold my tail close to my body, just in case.

There is a strip of sunlight snaking along the floor of the store, and I forget for just a moment where I am. I run, run, run and then . . . *smack!* As I dodge around a corner, I come face-to-face with the giant vacuum machine. The man with monkey ears lets out a cry and I release a screech and then we both just stand there. The machine growls and roars, hungry for my tail and tiara. Chipmunkey's little shout to "Get to the door!" reminds me that I'm just standing there, so I take off again.

"Knock, knock!" Chipmunkey cries happily when we get to the door. I push through it and scramble up into a tree to hide from the humans on the street below.

"Who's there?" I ask. I'm pretty sure I'm going to have to listen to a joke if I want Chipmunkey to tell me his idea for getting to Carter's school.

"A bus," Chipmunkey chatters.

"A bus who?"

"Not a buzzoo! A bus, for me and you!"

I groan. This is probably the worst joke yet— there is no such thing as a buzzoo. . . . Or is there? "What's a bus for me and you?" I ask.

"It's like a big, huge car. You're not going to believe how big it is. I've always wanted to take the bus, but I'm too short to climb up the first step. But you can carry me up the steps and we'll sit on a seat in the back and watch the world pass by. Oh boy oh boy oh boy, this is going to be so fun!"

At first, I think Chipmunkey's idea is silly. As

much as I want to see what this bus thing is all about, today is not about adventure—today, we need to stick to our mission. We need to find Lakeside Elementary so I can do what I came to the Human City to do and go home. But Chipmunkey looks so sure of himself that I can't help but trust him. "So we can definitely take the bus to Lakeside Elementary School? You can find the way?"

"Absolutely!" he declares proudly. "I watch human kids get on buses every day. I *know* where to go. You can trust me, Willa!"

I'm hopping and chattering, so excited about this new plan that I don't even realize that the bus is rolling down the street at that very moment. But Chipmunkey points and tells me what it is as it swooshes under us. He's right—a bus *is* a huge car. But instead of being yellow or blue or green like all the other cars, this bus has a picture of a polar bear painted on the side, and also a picture of a monkey that looks a lot like Sloth! It's an animal bus—we must be on the right track! It's a sign!

The bus is moving too quickly for me to jump on it as it goes past, so I hop out of the tree and run after it. I ignore the people that are pointing at me as I zip past on the sidewalk and run like crazy, hopping and swinging from the trees to keep up with the bus. "This bus will take us to Carter's school, I'm sure of it!" Chipmunkey cries.

The bus slows down for just a moment to let some Human Elders and a few little babies in through its side door. I hear the bus sigh to a stop, and that's all the time I need to hop from a branch onto its roof.

I sit proudly on the top of the giant bus, with my chipmunk friend settled in next to me. Chipmunkey and I are both so happy, watching the city pass by all around us. I lift my arms in the air and screech loudly, sure that if I stretch far enough I could touch the sky.

Does This Fit in Your Purse?

"Going somewhere?" Chipmunkey and I have been sitting on top of the bus for just a few short minutes when we're joined by a flapping flock of birds. The birds are gold and black, exactly like the doughnut-stealing bird at the zoo, and they sound just as snooty and rude.

The bird that asked us where we're going is perched on my tiara. Even though I'm shaking and twitching my body, I can't seem to get it to fly away. What is it with birds and tiaras? If this bird leaves a white streak on my pretty tiara... *grrr.*

"Yes," I answer proudly. "As a matter of fact, we're going to school."

"This bus doesn't go to school," another bird chants happily. "This bus is going to the zoo—didn't you see all the animals on the side? It's the *zoo* bus, silly."

"The zoo?" I ask, narrowing my eyes in disbelief. "Nuh-uh."

"It says so right there on the front of the bus," a third bird taunts. "Can't you *read*?"

I hear Chipmunkey growling behind me as he climbs back into the backpack. This is the first time I've heard him growl (at least, I think it's a growl . . . it's more like a sad, quiet rumble that's not at all threatening), which makes me think Chipmunkey likes birds about as much as I do.

A fourth bird—the last—has been gliding in the air next to us as the bus rumbles down the street. It finally lands alongside the other birds on the bus top and offers, "We can help you find your way to school, but you have to say, 'Birds are the prettiest and most brilliant beauties on this earth.'"

"Also," adds the bird sitting on my tiara, "please include the phrase, 'Birds make the world go round.'"

I hear Chipmunkey grumble, "Don't do it, Willa. We can figure this out on our own."

"I'm afraid we can't . . . ," I mutter back. "Unless you have another idea? I'm starting to think you don't really know where you're going."

"Well, now, I guess that might be true," Chipmunkey chatters. "But isn't the most important part the adventure in getting there?"

"Except I really want to find Carter today! It's the first day of school!" I cry, reaching my hand up to swat at the bird again. I wish the wind would blow the bird up into the air so it would have to stop pecking at the fur on my head. But instead of going faster, the bus we're on slows to a stop to let more people climb inside.

And that's when I realize something—none of the humans getting into this bus are kids like Carter. "Chipmunkey," I say quietly, because I don't want the birds to hear what I'm saying. "We need to find a bus with kids! Kids wearing backpacks would be on their way to school, right?"

I hear Chipmunkey squeak behind me, and then he says, "Willa! We need to find the yellow bus! Kids in backpacks ride the yellow bus! I remember now."

Just as the zoo bus starts to roll away from the sidewalk, a different bus creeps up behind us. It's yellow! I don't know what comes over me, but suddenly—desperate to get rid of the bird on my tiara and suddenly sure we're *really* on the right track—I leap from one bus onto the other. It's the longest jump I've ever landed, and I can't believe I actually made it.

The birds, who are obviously as startled as I am by my sudden switcheroo, are now fluttering in the air between the two buses. They squawk and screech as our yellow bus drives away and turns a corner to drive down a tree-lined street. Just as I start to get my breath back from the long leap, I see . . .

"Carter!" I can hardly believe it. But there he is, skipping down the street alongside a Human Elder. I am so excited that I start shouting and waving my arms and cackling. Heads turn at the sound of my screeching—I realize too late that everyone is looking at me *except* Carter.

When the bus slows enough to make it safe for me to leap off, I shimmy down the back of the bus and run along the sidewalk. I can't believe how close I am to the moment when I will give Carter his backpack and see his smile of gratitude. I'm bounding, hopping, and shouting, still trying to get Carter's attention. Finally, he notices me. I see his face flash with recognition—he knows who I am. I wave my arms and Carter points at me. He yells, "Look! My backpack!"

I spin in a circle, eager to show him that I kept his backpack safe. As I twirl and celebrate, just twenty jumps or so away from Carter, I hear a different human yell, "That monkey stole a boy's backpack! It's the monkey that escaped from the zoo!"

I did *not* steal Carter's backpack! I stop short in my tracks and spin around to protest.

Big mistake.

Because one minute, the sun is shining and I can smell the delicious notes of breakfast wafting through the early autumn air. The next, all light has been blotted out and my head is covered with something heavy and dark. It smells like apples and cinnamon, and despite my fear about what is happening to me, I get a little rumbling in my tummy from the scent of food temptations. My nose twitches and sniffs of its own free will.

"Smooth move," Chipmunkey murmurs from inside the backpack on my back. "This seems like a good time for a joke, to lighten the mood. What do you think?"

I sit down on the hard sidewalk, unable to take another step with the weight of this stinky dark curtain (or whatever it is) hanging over my head. I can feel human hands clutching clumsily at my body from outside the fabric and then—without warning—I'm flipped upside down.

There is a tiny howl as Chipmunkey falls from the open backpack on my back as we're whipped and flipped around. He's tiny enough to wiggle out of our captor's hands and out of the curtain that traps us. I can see him twist to land smoothly on his feet on the ground. He darts out of harm's way and I shout, "Run! Go find your family—I'll be fine. Carter will help me!"

Chipmunkey hops back and forth, unsure of what to do. But then he runs like crazy straight up into a tree, and I am relieved he's escaping. I hope I'll see him again sometime. I'll miss that little guy.

I'm sad that I don't even get to say good-bye, but my body is being squeezed and my hands are trapped tight inside the fabric wrapped around my fur. I can hear birds laughing up in the trees, which really doesn't help.

I finally come face-to-face with my captor, and I realize it's a human woman who has wrapped me in a giant bag and is holding me away from her at arm's length. It's as though she thinks I'm going to bite her, like some kind of animal—er, *mean* animal. Doesn't she see the tiara? I'm a true gentle princess on a mission to save a boy's backpack.

There are piles of stuff strewn on the sidewalk next to my captor—gum, beautiful headbands and jewels, and a small package of snacks—and I realize I must be lying at the bottom of this woman's now-empty purse. It's a big, huge purse.

Usually, I love purses—they're the source of most of the wonderful treasures that are dropped into the Monkey Pit. Human moms give children treats and prizes from their purses, and then they're dropped from those small human hands straight over the fence.

But *this* purse is rubbing all wrong on the soft fur on my back and squishing Carter's backpack against my skin in a most uncomfortable way. Also, I seem to be stuck. The human woman is squeezing me the way ZuZu clutches a banana, and I worry that I might be squished right out of my skin, like ZuZu's fruit always is. *Ouch!*

"She got him!" I hear someone shout from a few jumps away. "She caught the monkey that ran away from the zoo!"

The woman holding me won't look me in the eye, and I bet she's feeling sort of guilty for holding me so tightly. It's the same look the zoo doctors have when they're about to give us shots or do a checkup—they always look nervous and sorry. I chatter a bit to ask if maybe she could ease up, but this just makes her close the top of her purse over my head and zip it shut. Before she does, I see her eyeing my tiara. I hold it tight against my head, just in case she's considering taking it from me.

No one can hear me with my head stuffed inside this purse, and I wish with all my might that Carter would tell these people what happened. Just in time, I hear his tiny voice pipe up from somewhere near me and he says, "That's my backpack inside your purse, and that monkey is my friend."

"I am!" I shout from inside the purse. This inspires the woman to shake her purse violently. I don't think she likes when I talk to her. "Hey!" I shout, protesting the shaking. Then I push my arms and legs out against the edges of the purse to let her know I'm cramped in here. She shakes the bag again, and I decide it might be best if I just lie still and quiet for a little while. I'm starting to get motion sickness from this purse.

"Please, ma'am, can you let that monkey out of your bag?" Carter's voice is louder now. He must be standing close to us. I smile, despite the situation, and am grateful to him for being such a good friend.

I wait patiently for the purse to open up again, allowing me to climb out onto the sidewalk. The human woman will surely realize this is all a big mistake and let me out, once Carter explains everything. We'll all have a nice laugh about how she had me squeezed inside her purse for absolutely no reason at all. Maybe she'll apologize with a gift of some kind. I did like the look of that bright blue headband I saw lying on the sidewalk. . . .

But instead of the purse opening up, I feel myself thrown recklessly from one set of hands to another. Then a mean voice says, "This monkey is a runaway. The zoo's been looking all over for him, so he's coming with me."

Friends in High Places

"I'm not a he! I'm a girl!" I cry desperately, thrashing inside the purse. "Please, let me out of here! This is all a big misunderstanding. Carter, help!"

"We might need a tranquilizer," the menacing voice says.

"Noooooooooo!" I cry. I know all about tranquilizers. One time, Sloth threw a giant stick at Emily when she didn't bring enough food for lunch, and he had to get a special kind of shot that made him all oozy and slow. I do *not* want a tranquilizer near me.

I can feel a whole bunch of hands grasping at my body through the fabric of the purse, and I lay limp to show my human captors that I am very polite and calm. I guess it works, because the zipper on the purse slowly slides open so they can study me. When there is a hole just big enough for my head to poke through, I peek up and out quietly. A scary-looking human man is staring back at me with his ugly eyebrows pulled together.

And then I feel myself falling. *Wham!* I land on Carter's backpack inside the purse, but my backside still aches from hitting the sidewalk. At first, I don't realize what's happened. *Why did they drop me? Do I have bug breath?*

But when I look up, I see Chipmunkey peering down from the tree above us. He has a pile of acorns and pinecones that he is pushing off the branch straight onto my human captors' heads! Mr. Mean Voice is rubbing a big red bump on his nose. An acorn must have startled him so that he dropped me.

I take this opportunity to squirm right out of that purse. I squeeze myself through the tiny hole and run to Carter, who is only a few hops away. I wrap my arms around his leg and hold on for dear life. I am careful to be very, very gentle so as not to scare him—but he doesn't seem worried. He reaches down and pats my head affectionately. His hand knocks my tiara out of place, but I don't even care. All I can think about is keeping my arms wrapped tightly around his leg so the purse lady and Mr. Mean Voice can't take me again.

I look up into the tree at Chipmunkey, who is still shooting his tiny missiles down at the human captors. Chipmunkey lets out a long string of clucking cheers, and I know he is really enjoying himself. "Look, Willa!" he calls happily. "I'm just like Timothy!"

Chipmunkey still has a big pile—and his aim is much better than my brother's—so I'm pretty sure I'm safe letting go of Carter's leg for just a moment. It's time to finish the job I came here to do. I loosen one hand and pull the backpack strap off my right shoulder, then unhook the other side. I hold the backpack up toward Carter, and he bends down to take it from me.

"Did you come all the way from the zoo to bring this to me?" he asks, his eyes wide.

"Yes!" I shout happily. My smile is so big I think my face might split in two.

Carter smiles back at me and says, "I thought so! You are a pretty great monkey." Then he puts

the backpack on his back—right where it belongs. It fits him much better than it fits me. I'm feeling so happy until I realize that Chipmunkey has just thrown his last acorn, and the humans with the purse are coming toward me again. "Hold still, monkey," Mr. Mean Voice says.

As if I'm going to listen to anything this guy says! He threatened me with a tranquilizer! I unwrap my limbs from Carter's leg and stand behind my friend on the sidewalk, prepared to flee. But just before my feet can fly, Carter steps forward and says, "My grandma and I will make sure this monkey gets back to the zoo." He looks at me. "Is that okay with you?"

I nod vigorously and hop in place.

"Great!" Carter declares. Then he turns to the Human Elder that had been walking next to him. "Grandma, can I bring this monkey to school today?"

Carter's grandma looks at me carefully. She squints and bends down to gaze straight into my eyes. "Did you really come all the way here just to bring my Carter his backpack?" she asks.

I smile at her as nicely as I can, batting my eyes open and closed, the way I do when Emily brings a friend into the Monkey Pit. She laughs. "Well, you certainly are one smart monkey. Since you came all the way from the zoo just to find Carter, I think we can figure out a way to make this work. I'll call the zoo and tell them we have their monkey, safe and sound. We just need to make sure they're okay with the monkey taking a field trip—I'm sure they're worried about you, little guy."

I start to say, "I'm *not* a guy, check out the tiara," but decide to just hold my tongue. I don't really care if they think I'm a boy, especially if I get to go to Carter's school!

So I just smile and take Carter's hand in mine. He squeezes my hand back, and I see the birds fly away as Chipmunkey cheers up in the treetops. "Bye, Chipmunkey!" I yell up to him. "Thanks for the acorns! I'm going to miss you, friend!"

Show-and-Tell, Monkey Style!

I get to ride to Carter's school snuggled up inside a comfy crate that belongs to Carter's dog. The crate is propped inside a wagon, which Carter's grandma is pulling. I still don't exactly get what a dog is—and I'm pretty glad I don't have to find out, especially if Chipmunkey was right about the breath and the teeth.

But I *am* cool with sharing a dog's crate—once I get over the strange fur stench, which is like a stinky combination of wetness and pee. Mostly because there's a soft, fluffy blanket and Carter's grandma has filled the crate with fruit and nuts and other treats.

I bounce softly against the sides of the cage as Grandma pulls the rolling cart toward school. People are staring at me as we stroll down the sidewalk, so I smile and chatter, proud to be accompanied by humans that are as kind as Carter and his grandma.

A few people give me funny looks, and for them I reserve nice, loud raspberries and lip flutters that make them cluck their tongues and scowl at me. One especially mean-looking fellow is awarded a loud, roaring burp that smells like apples. I'm proud of that.

I'm so excited that I will get to see Lakeside Elementary School. I was a little nervous I might have to go straight back to the zoo, but Carter's grandma worked it out. I get to have a final adventure—on one condition. The zoo told Carter's grandma she had to get me cooped up, stat. I guess the zoo folks were worried about me running off to get ice cream or something.

But actually, being caged up is A-OK by me. Mostly because when I'm safe and sound in Carter's dog's carrying case, no one can steal my tiara. Carter told me I'm going to have to stay in this crate until the zookeepers come with the zoo van to pick me up. I guess that's what happens when you're a zoo monkey out and about in the Human City.

As we walk to school, Carter tells his grandma all about show-and-tell, and how he has the best thing ever to share with his classmates. I guess it's a good thing I got his gemstone back to him today, since he's really, really excited about showing it to his friends.

When we finally get to Lakeside Elementary, the first thing I see is a huge agility station in the yard. It's just like monkey school! Kids are jumping and leaping and throwing balls. . . . It looks so fun, and my whole body twitches and itches to get out of this cage to play and show them some of my moves. But Carter's grandma and I are hiding out in a corner of the play yard, and she asks me to stay really, really quiet. She says I get to surprise everyone later!

I realize this must be what it feels like for the humans at the zoo—they get to watch us play from their side of the fence, but they don't get to join in the fun. Maybe that's why the Human Elders look so grouchy sometimes—they just want to be in the Monkey Pit swinging, I guess.

Today, I'm a visitor at the Human Zoo in the city! Stuck behind a fence, observing and learning all about what humans can do. I'm going to watch carefully and tell ZuZu and Timothy about any cool human tricks that we haven't tried yet.

When a loud bell rings, all the kids run inside a giant building. "What's going on?" I ask Carter's grandma. "Why are we leaving school? Is it over already?" She doesn't answer. Instead, she pulls the wagon through a door and inside a funny building with a lot of rooms that remind me of indoor cages.

When Carter's grandma pulls my crate into something she calls "the classroom," all the kids come running up to peek at me. I smile and fluff my fur, telling them how happy I am to be there. Just when I think maybe it's time to get back outside so the lessons can start, all the kids sit in chairs and stare at a big wall at the front of the room.

"Hey, Grandma?" I ask quietly. "Why isn't anyone playing anymore?"

She shushes me, so I settle deeper into my blankets and watch what's happening. I look around the classroom and see tubs filled with brightly colored sticks and papers. There are books and pictures of giant beasts on the walls. *Ooh! Ooh!* I think I see a picture of a seal!

Even though there are a ton of really cool things to look at, human school is very strange. There are no jumping lessons—in fact, one kid named Jasmine is *scolded* for hopping out of her chair!—and everyone mostly just sits still. Sitting still all day just can't compare to Air Acrobatics. All I can think is, *I'm glad I go to Monkey School!*

The room is very quiet, so I'm starting to drift off to sleep when I spot Carter walking toward the back of the room to visit me. He's carrying a piece of paper and a colored stick. He shows me how you use the stick to make marks on the paper, then pushes the paper through the door of the crate for *me* to play with! It's just like the lipstick Chipmunkey and I used on our bodies in the store last night, but this color stick also draws on paper!

I lift it toward my lips to draw on them and show Carter what I learned at the store last night. But when the stick gets close to my mouth, Carter whispers, "Don't eat it! That's a crayon, monkey." And then he laughs. "If the zoo people say it's okay, I'm going to give you some crayons to take back to the zoo, so you can share them with your friends at Monkey School." I push my lips out into a kissy face and it makes a big raspberry noise. Carter giggles, then heads back to his chair while I test out the color stick.

My paper is almost covered with color when I hear the teacher say it's time for show-and-tell. Now, this is what I've been waiting for! I'm so glad the zoo van didn't get here to pick me up before show-and-tell. I can't wait to see everyone's treasures!

The teacher tells Carter he can go first. And guess what? *I'm* his show-and-tell. Carter's precious rock stays hidden, deep down at the bottom of his backpack, and instead Carter wheels *me*—Princess Willoughby Wallaby Fluff!—up to the front of the classroom and tells them all about how we met and how I saved his backpack. He tells his friends I'm a hero!

I hold up my pretty drawing to show Carter's friends the picture I colored, and everyone cheers. The teacher gives me a box of crayons and a whole bunch of paper that she says I can take back to the zoo. I can't wait to show ZuZu what I got for him! This is *way* better than ice cream, I'm sure of it.

Then all the kids make faces at me and pretend to be monkeys, and the teacher tells them they will spend next week in school learning all about monkeys. "And maybe," she says with a friendly smile, "we can go visit Carter's monkey friend at the zoo very, very soon!"

As Carter smiles and holds my hand through the wall of the crate, I decide I've never felt more special and prized in my life.

The Treasure Team

The sun is bright overhead as the zookeepers walk me through the zoo later that day. My insides start to get all squirmy when I can see the tippy-top branches of the tickling tree. *I'm almost home!*

I hear the shouts of my friends and family as they jump and hop around the Monkey Pit, playing and learning. I hear Fred Astaire's rough voice, barking instructions to his class, and I remember that today is the first day of school—I'm late!

"*Ooh! Ooh!*" I cry. "Madame Rose Marie Osmond is going to be so mad at me."

I know I'll have to make up for my missed first

day of class with extra swinging practice every day for a while. But that's okay, because my adventure was worth it. And you know what? After dealing with Frank the rat and the man with the broom and the purse lady and Mr. Mean Voice, even Madame Rose Marie Osmond's firm hand doesn't scare me anymore!

But I start to fidget anyway, nervous that maybe other monkeys will be mad at me and not talk to me. That would be terrible! Will they welcome me back? Is everyone going to be upset that I left the Pit?

We get to enter the Monkey Pit through the human door that Emily uses to deliver our meals, and I notice that everyone has turned to stare as these strange zookeepers walk into the Monkey Pit with a carrying cage in their hand. No one knows it's me in here, and my fur is beginning to itch because I'm so hot. They open the front of the crate and I step timidly out onto the familiar dirt. I inhale deeply, catching the scent of bananas in the air.

And then, in just an instant, I'm surrounded. My mom flies over faster than I've ever seen her move and she sweeps me up into a hug so hard that I lose my breath. Her tail wraps around my body, and I can feel her sniffing my shoulders, my arms, and my head. "Oh, Miss Fluff!" she mutters quietly. I hear a low growl rolling out from beneath the loving embrace, and know I'll need to give her a lot of kisses and cuddling to make up for my escape.

"Willa!" I hear ZuZu call to me from way across the Pit in the Air Acrobatics course. He swings expertly from branch to branch and lands at my feet. His grin is a mile wide, and he's jumping and screeching happily. Timothy is clucking at me from up in our family branch, and I wave my arms in the air when he shows me the tricks he's already learned during the first day of school.

I'm so happy to be home, and I can't wait to tell everyone about my adventure and everything I saw in the Human City. But the very first thing I have to do is share presents! I reach inside the carrying crate and take out the paper and the crayons that Carter and his teacher gave to me. All of my friends and classmates circle around, and I show everyone how to use them. They all hoot and hop and reach for the magic crayons, eager to color pictures.

Timothy is still up in the tree, practicing his new tricks. I hear him shout, "Watch this, Willa!" I turn just in time to see him slip as he does a swing jump, and he falls on his backside. I open my arms and he sneaks up to hug me.

He cuddles in against my fur for a comforting snuggle, then peeks past me to see how the crayons work. I give him the prettiest, most wonderful crayon that I saved just for him—the one that Carter called "burnt umber" that makes me think about the stripe that runs down Chipmunkey's tail. I know Timothy will love to hear all of my stories about Chipmunkey—I bet they would be great friends.

"Thanks, Willa," he says quietly. "I really missed you. I didn't have anyone to throw my grapes at this morning—you make the funniest faces, so it's not as fun to launch them at other people."

My mom, who is still standing right beside me, begins to growl a little louder. I decide I'd better take out her present now. I reach into the crate one last time and pull out the extra-special treasure that Carter's grandma gave me just as I was leaving school.

Grandma told me I deserved a prize for bringing Carter his backpack, and she thought I would like her pretty scarf to go with my beautiful tiara. It is so beautiful—the most magical treasure I've ever seen—but as soon as she gave it to me, I just knew it would be perfect for my mom. It's pink and marvelous and I want her to have it, more than I've ever wanted anything for myself.

So I hold the scarf delicately in my arms and turn to give it to my mom. "This is for you, Mom. I'm sorry I left the Monkey Pit."

Even though I can tell Mom loves the scarf—and it looks absolutely beautiful draped over her head—she still looks angry. "I appreciate the gift, Willa, but I want you to know that this doesn't make me any less upset with you."

"I know," I murmur, nuzzling in against her with a hug.

"And you're absolutely *not* getting that purple earring back, no matter what."

I nod. "I know." ZuZu must have told her about my plan. I'll forgive him for that.

Then she smiles at me, and even though I know I'm in big fat trouble, it will be okay. She says, "I was afraid something might have happened to

143

you—you've never been outside the Monkey Pit, and I didn't know what kind of trouble might have found you out there. Never again, under any circumstances, are you to go up to the ledge again. That means no more treasure collecting—do you understand?"

"Yes, Mom," I agree. I don't even cross my arms this time. As I'm hugging her to show that I really, truly mean it, I hear a loud clucking chatter from up near the ledge.

I look up. *"Ooh, ooh!* Chipmunkey!" I call happily, seeing my little chipmunk friend stretching up to put his front paws on the fence that runs along the top edge of the Monkey Pit. I give my mom one more squeeze, then break away from her embrace so I can climb up to the top of the tickling tree. That's when I see that *all* the chipmunks are with Chipmunkey, standing in a line. Each one is sitting on its haunches, chewing a snack.

"Hi, Willa!" Chipmunkey calls. All the other chipmunks repeat his greeting before turning back to their snacks. I feel ZuZu's tail wrap around me as he sits down next to me on the branch, and I nuzzle in close. It feels *perfect* to be sitting with him in the tickling tree, and I don't have even the tiniest urge to crawl over the fence to join Chip-munkey and his friends on their adventure.

Chipmunkey skitters back and forth in front of the fence. "Guess what, Willa? I'm not a city chip anymore! Now that I'm officially a chip*munkey*, we have decided we'd like to come live by you at the zoo!"

"That's great!" I cry. "I can't wait to introduce you to all my friends. This is my best friend, ZuZu." ZuZu hops in greeting, and Chipmunkey chatters and twitches his tail.

"How did you get here?" I ask. The zoo is a long way from the city, and chipmunks have such tiny legs for running.

"We took the zoo bus!" he cries proudly. "We learned from you. . . . All the chipmunks waited on a branch over the road, and when the bus with a picture of a monkey and a polar bear stopped to pick up the people standing under us, we just hopped right on! Chipmunkeys are very smart, don't you think? Oh, hey . . . I have a new joke. Wanna hear it?"

"Yes!" ZuZu cries, before I can warn him that he does *not* want to hear any of Chipmunkey's jokes.

"Knock, knock!"

"Who's there?" I answer.

"Monkey!"

"Monkey who?" ZuZu asks, grinning.

"Monkey see, monkey zoo, that's who!" Chipmunkey yells. "It rhymes! Isn't that a good one, Willa?"

ZuZu looks at me, and then we both start laughing, even though the joke wasn't really a joke and wasn't at all funny. "I'm glad you're here, Chipmunkey," I admit.

Chipmunkey darts back and forth, busy and silly as always. "Listen, Willa, we're actually here to do a job, so no time to talk." He rubs his little paws together and exhales a long trilling sound.

"A job?" ZuZu asks. "What kind of job?"

Chipmunkey looks proud. "Chipmunkeys are a special brand of monkey, as you obviously know." He tucks his little nose down and pushes something toward the edge of the fence. I see something shiny peek under the fence and roll onto the ledge. Whatever it is keeps rolling and falls to the ground in the Monkey Pit. "We brought you a little present. Go check it out!"

I scramble down the tree trunk and collect a

shiny object from the ground. I climb back up into the tree to sit beside ZuZu before opening my hand to find out what it is. "It's a color stick—the lipstick kind!" I cheer. "Pink!"

"We know how much you love treasures, Willa," Chipmunkey says happily. "So we've decided to appoint ourselves as the zoo's all-new Treasure Team!"

"The Treasure Team?" I ask, blinking wide eyes.

"We, the noble chipmunkeys, are here to help you. We don't want you to get in trouble for going up to the ledge again, so we are going to bring the very best treasures to you!"

"You would do that for me?" I ask. "You'll bring treasures from the Human Zoo to the Monkey Pit? Can I share them with my friends during a show-and-tell at my school?"

Chipmunkey nods his tiny little head, and all the other chipmunks start nodding, too. "The mighty chipmunkeys, the official Treasure Team, are at your service! So . . . who wants ice cream?"

I look at ZuZu and grin like crazy.

You know what's really great about the Monkey Pit? I can be me, and I can be as loud and crazy as I want to be without worrying about getting chased with a broom or a purse. And that's a good thing, since as soon as I put some of the glittery pink color stick on ZuZu's lips, I can't stop myself from laughing and jumping and screeching happily.

And even as a mushy grape comes flying at me from my brother's stinky palm, all I can think is, *It's good to be home.*

Erin Soderberg does not throw grapes. But, like Willa, she does like to swing, climb trees, and relax by the lake reading and listening to stories. She is the author of several other books for kids and teens, which were written under a different name. ("Soderberg" is her monkey alias!) Erin lives in Minneapolis, Minnesota, with her husband and three little kids—who do throw grapes.

Here's a sneak peek at

The Pup Who Cried Wolf

Into the Heart of Wolf Country

Anyone with a good nose and a wild heart can feel the change. I know it the moment we cross the line. Wilderness. I can feel it in my teeth.

Also it helps that there is a big wooden sign that says YELLOWSTONE NATIONAL PARK, and a Yellowstone National Park ranger station with a sign that says YELLOWSTONE NATIONAL PARK RANGER STATION. And the other thing that helps me figure out where we are is the ranger who comes out to the car and says, "Welcome to Yellowstone National Park."

Somehow.

Someway.

Leash or no leash, I am going to escape.

The ranger sounds all friendly, but he turns out to be a rude sort. "Oh, a killer dog," he says when he sees me. He tells Mona to keep the windows up as soon as we leave the ranger station. He probably knows I'll hate that. He says don't feed the bears. Then he mentions some silly law. "Keep your dog on a leash at all times inside the park."

Umm, how am I going to meet my wolf pack on a leash?

"Usually we say that to protect the smaller wildlife such as squirrels." The ranger is still talking. "But in his case, the squirrels might just mistake him for one of their babies that fell out of the tree, carry him back upstairs, and stuff him full of nuts."

Ha, ha, ha. Oh boy. I am so done with this guy. I give him a taste of my rapid-fire barking to show what I think of him.

"Keep the noise down," he says. "Otherwise, I'll have to get out my flyswatter."

Mona starts laughing, and Glory, who has been quiet up till now, starts giggling. And then I hear a snigger. Heckles. That's it. I'm finished with this family and ready to find my pack.